# Contents

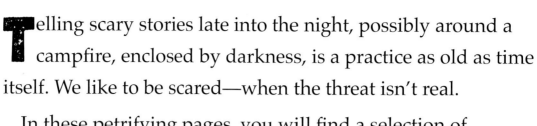elling scary stories late into the night, possibly around a campfire, enclosed by darkness, is a practice as old as time itself. We like to be scared—when the threat isn't real.

In these petrifying pages, you will find a selection of brand-new stories and retellings of famous urban legends.

We have given each story a "scare rating" out of 5:

If the scares get too much, you can choose a story with a lower rating that will calm you down.

But be warned, at the back of the book you will find our scariest, most terrible of tales in the Nightmare Fuel chapter.

These hair-raising horror stories have been especially written to be read aloud, like at a campout or a slumber party, and definitely in the dark.

## How to Read Scary Stories to an Audience

Read quietly, filling your voice with dread. Make your voice louder as the danger increases and, should there be a cliffhanger, drag out the final sentence, letting the scares hang in the air over your audience and sending chills down their spines.

We hope you enjoy reading our tales of terror out loud or to yourself. Don't say we didn't warn you.

# CHAPTER 1
# Unsolved Mysteries & Uninvited Guests

# Footsteps in the Roof

## SCARE RATING

Ollie sat bolt upright in bed, listening to the unmistakable sound of footsteps coming from the ceiling crawlspace above his head. He and his dad lived in an old house on the outskirts of town— their closest neighbor was a mile away. The footsteps stopped, but Ollie's heart kept pounding.

"I heard something in the roof last night," Ollie told his dad.

"Probably just a rat," Dad said, busily tapping on his phone.

"It sounded bigger than a rat," Ollie insisted.

The next day, Ollie came home from school during his lunch break, having forgotten to feed the cat, Shadow, that morning. But when he got there, he found Shadow eating fresh cat food; her water bowl filled to the brim.

"Hello! Anyone there!?" Ollie shouted, but the house was silent.

A few days later, Ollie reached for his comic book from the bedside table, but it was missing. Weird. Dad was out, so he couldn't ask him if he had taken it.

Later, Ollie opened the fridge and reached for a can of soda.

There were two cans missing from yesterday. Ollie had refilled the fridge just last night. Double weird! Dad *hated* soda.

When he returned to his bedroom, his comic had been put back on the bedside table. Only, the bookmark was

on a different page and dark fingerprints smudged the pages. He glanced in the closet door mirror and felt his hair stand on end—the hatch to the ceiling crawlspace was open. Behind him, the door clicked shut and the lock turned from inside the room.

"I've been watching you for a while," a low voice said in his ear.

# Destination Unknown

## SCARE RATING 💀 💀

Tadashi sat up in the train cab as his dad prepared the train for its four-hour trip to Tokyo. He watched in awe as Dad turned the ignition and pulled the lever to start the train moving down

the tracks. Tadashi wanted to be a driver, too, when he was older. As the night wore on, Tadashi curled up in his seat, his eyes growing heavy. It was cold outside, and snow was falling.

"You want to drive?" Dad asked, and Tadashi was immediately awake.

Dad's steady hand guided his son's on the lever, and Tadashi felt proud to be able to keep the train running smoothly.

He squinted into the snowy night. In the distance, a figure was walking in the field. But who would be out so late in a snowstorm?

"Dad, look!" he said.

As they sped closer, Tadashi could see it was a woman, dressed in a long black coat, and she was walking steadily toward the tracks.

Dad hit the horn, sending a blast of noise into the frozen night, but the woman paid it no attention. Dad pushed Tadashi aside and grabbed the emergency brake, pulling on it with all his strength.

"We're going to hit her!" Dad cried. "Hold tight, Tadashi!"

But as the train squealed to a shuddering halt, sparks flying, the woman passed right through the train, unhurt, like she was made of air.

Tadashi turned to his father and blinked in shock. He stuck his head out the train window, looking for the woman, but there was only a long, black coat, billowing on the tracks.

# Spotlight Through the Window

## SCARE RATING

A bright light shined on Fiona's face as she lay in bed. Groggily, she sat up and peered out the window to see a shiny metal object hovering in the night sky, its beam pointed right at her. Eyes widening with fright, Fiona called out to her brother Pete, who was in his bed across the room.

"What's up?" he said sleepily, as she pointed to the strange, gleaming object.

Then it vanished in a blink.

"I can't see anything," Pete said.

Pete quickly fell back to sleep, but Fiona stayed by the window. The object returned, hovering above her house, then disappeared again. It didn't look like an airplane. Could it be a . . .

Could it really be a spaceship?

The light snapped back on and filled the room like a spotlight. Fiona felt her body rise up and float through the air, toward the open window. Toward the ship. She struggled against the beam, but she was trapped and floating quickly toward an open hatch at the base of the hovering craft.

Once inside the ship, a tall, thin figure appeared. Its skin was pale green and its long, webbed fingers caressed her forehead. It peered down at her with curious black eyes. A needle jabbed into her arm and Fiona passed out.

When she woke, Fiona was back in her bed. What a weird nightmare. It had felt so real . . .

"Wake up, Fiona! We'll be late for school!" Pete shouted at her.

Fiona struggled to get out of bed; she was so thirsty, and her head throbbed in pain. Pete looked at her in horror, his eyes wide.

"F . . . Fiona?" he stammered.

Fiona examined herself in the mirror, gasping at her reflection. Her hair had grown down past her waist and she looked at least a year older. Her arms were covered in needle marks and when she spoke, her words came out in an alien language. Her eyes, once pale blue, were now black slits.

## SCARY BUT TRUE!

A UFO (Unidentified Flying Object) is sighted somewhere in the world every six minutes! UFOs are often described as oval or disc shaped with bright lights and strange flying patterns.

# The Artist's Studio

## SCARE RATING 💀 💀 💀

Marco couldn't believe his new artist's studio had once belonged to the great master, Nazario. Hundreds of years ago, before the artist went mad and cut off his own middle finger, Nazario had worked in this exact cramped, dusty room at the top of the art school. He had produced his masterpieces right here, at Marco's workbench.

Marco wanted to be as famous as Nazario and he was spending his summer vacation in Tuscany, working on his own exhibition of paintings.

Looking out to the view of the rolling hills, vines, and red-roofed farmhouses, Marco splashed golds, blues, and greens on the canvas. He felt like Nazario was there with him, guiding his brush. Marco worked until the sun set and his fingers cramped. Reluctantly, at the end of each day he packed up his paints and brushes and locked the studio behind him.

In the morning, Marco opened up the door to find his paints

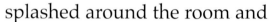

splashed around the room and all his brushes missing. He searched every corner, every drawer, and the entire room for the brushes, but they were nowhere to be found. Turning to his painting on the easel, Marco gasped in shock—it had been slashed with a knife and splattered with black paint. All his hard work was ruined!

Marco heard an evil laugh from somewhere in the room. He spun around, terrified, as an open can of red paint somehow tipped over, spilling crimson liquid across the worn wooden floor.

In the paint, a handprint appeared . . . and it was missing the middle finger.

## SCARY BUT TRUE!

At the end of the 19th century, séances (contacting the dead through a guide known as a medium) were very popular and unscrupulous mediums featured the use of a paranormal ghost slime called ectoplasm, tilting tables, and levitation to trick their customers.

# Talking to Strangers

## SCARE RATING

"I'm bored—let's do a séance," my cousin Natalie said, like she'd said a hundred times over the summer. It was raining outside, so we couldn't go to the beach.

"Okay," I agreed.

She got out her ouija board: a cardboard rectangle printed with the alphabet, numbers from 1 to 10, and boxes saying YES and NO. She put the plastic pointer on the board and we placed our fingers on it. This was stupid. We'd done a bunch of séances before and nothing ever happened. I stifled a yawn.

"We gather here in the hopes of receiving a spirit," Natalie said dramatically. "Is anyone out there?"

The pointer moved, very slowly, toward **YES**.

"Are you moving it?" Natalie whispered.

I shook my head, starting to feel nervous.

"What's your name?" I asked the spirit.

The pointer spelled out: **ROSE WHITE. MURDERED. 1959.**

Natalie widened her eyes at me. Everyone in town knew the sad story of Rose White, a young girl who had vanished from a beach party in the 1950s. Her disappearance had never been solved.

"Cut it out, Lucy," Natalie whispered.

"I'm not doing anything!" I insisted.

The table shook underneath us, and the lights flickered, then went out. We both screamed.

"What do you want, Rose?" Natalie asked, tears streaming down her cheeks.

The pointer moved slowly to more letters. **YOU**

I upended the board, jumped up, and turned the lights back on.

"I don't want to do this anymore, Natalie!" I cried. "It's too scary!"

Natalie turned to me, the pupils of her eyes had turned white, and she had an odd smile on her face.

"I'm not Natalie. I'm Rose."

# Not on My Watch

## SCARE RATING 💀💀💀

"Your grandad wanted you to have this," said George's mother. "Hold out your arm."

She strapped the antique silver watch around George's wrist.

"Do I have to wear it?" George complained.

He wanted a smartwatch, not this clunky relic, and he hadn't even liked his grandad much; he had been cranky and mean.

"Your grandfather wore it every day for fifty years. He wanted you to have it."

George wore the watch for a few days, then he slipped it into a box and hid it in his closet and forgot all about it.

One morning, months later, he woke up and lifted his arm—the watch was back on his wrist! George ran down the hall, furious.

"Mom! I don't want to wear Grandad's watch! Why did you put it back on me while I was sleeping?"

"I didn't touch the watch," Mom said, her eyes widening.

George flung the watch on the tile floor, accidentally smashing the glass face.

Reluctantly, he took it to a repair shop.

"This is a classic," said the repair guy. "I bet it's worth a fortune."

"You want it?" George said. "I'll sell it to you."

The next day, George got a phone call from the repair guy.

"You know that watch you sold me, I can't find it anywhere. Did you come back for it?"

"No," said George, a chill running through his body.

He felt something tighten on his wrist. He looked down to see the straps of Grandad's watch getting tighter and tighter, until his hand turned blue.

# Tea for Two

## SCARE RATING 💀

Madeline loved her new house, especially the rope swing that hung from the oak tree in the yard, and the little treehouse above it. Her elderly neighbor had said that, many years ago, a little girl with flaming-red hair built the treehouse with her father and played in it for hours.

One morning, Madeline found her mom standing in the kitchen with a puzzled look on her face.

"Two of my china teacups are missing," she said. "Did you take them?"

"Nope," Madeline said.

"I suppose they'll turn up, maybe we haven't unpacked them."

The following day, Mom knocked on Madeline's bedroom door.

"I can't find my picnic blanket, have you seen it?" she asked.

Madeline shook her head and wondered if Mom was getting forgetful as she got older.

The day after that, Madeline snuck into the pantry and reached into the cookie jar, disappointed to find just crumbs. It had been full to the brim with fresh chocolate chip cookies—her favorite—only yesterday.

Her tummy rumbling, she wandered out to the treehouse, climbing the ladder to the small room in the branches.

From the window, she saw a little girl with red hair sitting on the picnic blanket, sipping on imaginary tea. The picnic was set for two and each plate was laden with cookies. The girl smiled and waved, but as Madeline ducked her head and crawled through the small door, the girl vanished. All she left behind was the afternoon tea and a strand of ginger-colored hair.

# CHAPTER 2

# It Happened to a Friend of a Friend of Mine...

# Killer in the Backseat

## SCARE RATING

The deserted road is pitch black and slippery with rain after the storm. All around is nothing but thick forest for miles. As I drive down the old highway, back from my high school basketball game, out of nowhere a truck drives up behind my car. I wave out the window for the driver to pass, but he inches closer, tailgating and flashing blinding high beams into my back window. I fight to keep my eyes on the road, panic rising.

What's this guy's problem? I slow down but he moves even closer to my bumper, nearly touching it, still flashing his lights at me. My breathing quickens with fear. Is he trying to run me off the road?

He rams my bumper hard and I nearly skid into the guardrail and down a steep ravine. Again, he flashes his lights on and off, blinding me. My knuckles turn white as I grip the wheel. My phone is in the backseat, I never usually put it there—what was I thinking?

My tires screech and I slide on the slick road as I make a hard turn off the highway, almost losing control. The driver holds down his horn but passes by, his taillights fading into the darkness. I drive slowly, carefully, the rest of the way home. I'm shaking like a leaf as I park in the driveway of my house. There are no lights on; my parents must still be out.

As I take off my seatbelt, I feel a tickle on the back of my neck, like fingers playing with my hair.

A low whisper makes me freeze.

"He was just trying to warn you."

In the rear-vision mirror, I see a man in a ghost mask in the backseat, a sharp knife glinting in his hand.

# The Black-eyed Children

## SCARE RATING

I wait in the car, bored, while Mom is in the store. It's dinner time and already pitch black outside. What's taking her so long? I yawn and let my head rest on the car seat, nodding off. A loud knock on the driver's side window startles me awake.

21

Two boys, one older, one younger, with pale white skin and hoodies pulled over their heads stand by the car, staring blankly at me. "We need a ride. Will you let us in?" asks one of the boys.

A cold chill runs through me. Something about the pair isn't right.

"No way," I say. Were they serious? "My mom will be back soon."

"We're just kids; we need a ride," pleads the older boy.

I don't want to let them in, but I move my hand slowly to unlock the car. As I'm about to flip the lock and let them inside, I glance up at the boys' faces one more time and my breath catches in my throat. Their eyes are black as ink. No irises. No pupils.

"We can't come in unless you tell us it's okay," says the older boy.

I remove my hand from the door lock.

"*Let us in!*" shouts the smaller boy, slamming both palms on the window.

I turn toward the store for help and see Mom wheeling her cart toward me, unaware. I wave frantically at her, while the boys bang hard on the windows. When I look back, the noise stops and just like that, the black-eyed boys are gone.

## SCARY BUT TRUE!

There are lots of urban legends about alligator sightings in very strange places, like sewers and drains, especially in big cities such as New York. People say it's because baby reptiles have been flushed down the toilet by their owners and have then grown into huge, monstrous beasts underground.

# The Hookman

## SCARE RATING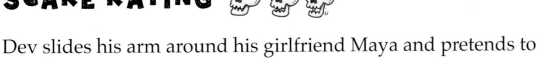

Dev slides his arm around his girlfriend Maya and pretends to be interested in the sweeping views of Lovers Lane lookout.

"It's so beautiful up here," says Maya, as Dev goes in for a kiss.

The romantic music on the car radio abruptly cuts out and Maya pushes him away.

"In breaking news," the announcer says, "a convicted killer has escaped from Bay City correctional facility this morning, and is still at large."

Maya sits up straight, suddenly feeling very isolated at the lookout.

"What did he say?" she asks. There's no one around tonight; it's just Dev and Maya, overlooking the city lights.

"He could be armed and is very dangerous," the announcer continues. "Residents in the area should stay inside if possible. The man is described as six feet tall, wearing an orange jumpsuit with a hook prosthesis on his right arm."

Dev pulls Maya closer to him, peering into the darkness, and locks the car doors. His pulse is racing now. They're only a few miles from the high-walled maximum-security prison. The murderer could be behind any tree; jump out from any bush.

"Let's go home," he says.

Maya nods, her face pale. Dev tries to start the car, but the engine won't turn over. The radio ran the battery flat.

"No!" Dev says, panicking. He punches the steering wheel with frustration.

They both hear a noise that makes the hair on the back of their necks stand on end.

A metallic sound scrapes along the roof of the car, inches above their heads.

"Start the car!" screams Maya.

Dev desperately turns the key and pumps the accelerator. The engine roars to life and the couple speed back home, filled with relief.

Maya climbs out of the car and slams the door. But then she lets out a scream of terror: embedded in the front passenger door is a hook.

# The Licked Hand

## SCARE RATING

There's a weird sound coming from outside my window, a steady *crunch, crunch, crunch.* What could it be? I think about getting up to investigate, but I'm too sleepy and warm to move.

The floorboards creak underneath my bed and I reach down to where my dog, Rufus, sleeps. He licks my hand and I smile; he always makes me feel safe at night.

"Good dog," I whisper.

Rufus keeps licking my hand, his doggy breath rasping until I fall asleep.

The next morning, the strange sound outside is still there. *Crunch, crunch, crunch.* I get out of bed and pull the blinds open.

To my surprise, on the patio outside, Rufus sees me and whimpers in the chill air, a well-chewed lamb bone at his feet. If Rufus was outside all night . . . what was licking my hand?

# Charlie and the Slender Man

## SCARE RATING 💀💀💀💀

My kid brother Charlie is playing on the swings at the playground, when I see a tall, thin man standing motionless at the tree line nearby. He's *really* tall, like seven feet, and wearing a black suit, even though it's the middle of summer. I can't quite make out his face, but I can tell he's watching Charlie play. I sit up, my eyeballs bulging. The man is beckoning to Charlie and he has a candy bar in his hand . . . no, it's not a hand, it's a tentacle!

"Charlie, no!" I leap up as Charlie starts skipping towards the man. He loves chocolate. I sprint across the park, panicking about what this creep might do next.

"Hey!" I shout at the guy. "Leave my brother alone!"

As I get closer to the man, I slow to a stop, unable to believe my eyes. His face points toward me; his blank, featureless face. I inhale sharply; this isn't a man, it's a monster! It turns its attention back to Charlie, my brother scoffing the candy bar. The man scoops up Charlie, cradling him in his long arms, and carries him away into the trees.

"Stop!" I shout again.

I run as hard as I can after them, struggling for air, but I can't keep up—the man's legs are twice as long as mine. As they disappear into the misty woods, Charlie lets out a blood-curdling scream.

## SCARY BUT TRUE!

'Creepypastas' aren't a menu item at a Halloween-themed restaurant, they're spooky horror tales and legends that are copied and pasted and shared around the internet. They often seem real, but they're not. Mostly.

# The Vanishing Hitchhiker

## SCARE RATING

Murray's dad drove carefully through the thick fog. With the hazard lights on, his dad was driving *so slowly*, so they didn't run off the coastal road straight down into the rocky bay. Ahead of them in the mist, Murray spotted a lone hitchhiker on the road. A young girl with dark, plaited hair, wearing a long, tattered white dress, her thumb out for a ride. She was barefoot and looked a mess.

"Dad, let's stop and pick her up," Murray begged, not wanting the girl to spend the night on the dangerous road. "She's all alone."

His dad slowed the car, pulling off to the side, and Murray buzzed down his window, glad they could rescue her. But as the girl walked toward them, he got a sinking feeling in the pit of his stomach. Her face was pale and gaunt and her dress had dark stains on it. Was that . . .

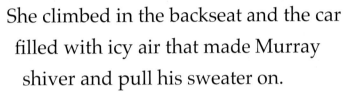

She climbed in the backseat and the car filled with icy air that made Murray shiver and pull his sweater on.

"My parents will be waiting for me," the girl said in an eerie whisper. "I live at 22 Rose Lane."

Murray tried to make conversation with the girl on the drive, but he was glad when she fell fast asleep. As they arrived at the girl's house, Murray turned his head and couldn't believe his eyes. The backseat was empty, and the girl had vanished.

Still wanting to tell her family that they had seen the girl, Murray and his dad knocked on the door of the house, and an old lady appeared. When they asked if a young girl with dark braids lived in the house, the woman clutched at her chest in shock.

"My daughter had long dark hair, but she died many years ago. She was killed by a hit-and-run driver on the Coast Highway . . . She was wearing a long white dress."

**SCARY BUT TRUE!**

Cry-baby Bridges are bridges reportedly haunted by the ghosts of children and babies. At one bridge in Blackstone, Virginia, baby cries are heard, and if you stop on the bridge and sprinkle baby powder on the hood of your car, small footprints may appear in the powder!

# Have you Checked the Children?

## SCARE RATING

The Singhs' two kids Arya and Saanjh have been asleep for hours and I'm trying to stay awake by watching late-night TV until their parents come home. When the phone rings from the kitchen I jump out of my skin, suddenly wide awake. Who would be calling this late?

I pick up the call, worried sick.

"Have you checked the children?" a man's deep, monotone voice asks down the line.

"Who is this?" I ask, terrified.

It didn't sound like Mr Singh . . . but who else would want to know?

The man ended the call and I immediately lock all the doors, mute the TV and listen carefully, but the house is silent; the children sleeping soundly. I sit nervously on the couch, my heart hammering.

The phone rings again, and although I don't want to answer it, I do.

"Have you checked the children?" the deep voice says again.

I stab the end call button and immediately call the police.

They say they'll put a trace on the next call to find out where it's coming from.

"Keep him on the line for as long as you can," the policewoman says.

I stand at the bottom of the staircase, staring up toward the children's bedroom, frozen to the spot, not sure what I should do.

The phone rings again and my whole body jumps. My hand trembles as I answer the call.

"I told you to check the children," the man says, "and you haven't."

"How . . . how do you know?" I ask, hardly able to speak.

I hear a muffled laugh from the other end.

I end the call, my heart in my throat, and within seconds the police call me back.

"The call is coming from inside the house! Get out now!"

I drop the phone and race up the stairs to the kids' room, dreading what I might find. Heavy footsteps follow me up the stairs . . .

# The Clown in the Corner

## SCARE RATING

House-sitting for my aunt and uncle is a piece of cake. After I water the plants, feed the cat, and take the garbage out, all that's left to do is watch TV in the basement. I take a bowl of popcorn downstairs, flick on the big screen, and put my feet up to watch a movie.

It seems their taste in décor has changed since the last time I visited; in the corner of the room stands a life-size clown statue. I've been afraid of clowns since I was a little kid, and this one is particularly unsettling. It's so real-looking: tall, with curly purple hair, a white painted face, slick red lips, and an oversized bow tie.

I try to concentrate on the movie, but I can't shake the feeling that the clown statue is watching me.

I pick up my phone, turn my back on the unsettling clown, and call my uncle. He picks up right away; it sounds like he's at a party.

"Hey Chris! How's everything going at the house?" he shouts.

"Hi! Um, sorry to bother you, Uncle Henry, but I was wondering . . . could I move the clown statue in the basement into the cupboard? It's erm, nice and all, but it's kinda creeping me out."

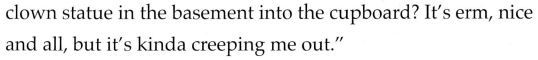

My uncle is silent for a moment, and I can hear him move to a quieter room.

"Chris, buddy, what are you talking about?" he says, his voice serious. "*What* clown statue?"

"The big, life-size one in the basement," I say.

"We don't have a clown statue," Uncle Henry says, and my blood runs cold. "Get out of the house, now!"

My heart pounding, I look back at the clown statue, but it's no longer in the corner.

That's when a yellow-gloved hand taps my shoulder.

"Wanna play?"

# CHAPTER 3
# Ghosts & Ghouls

# Caught on Camera

## SCARE RATING

As Jack does his homework at the kitchen counter, the doorbell rings twice.

"Are you expecting anyone?" his mom asks, checking the clock. It's exactly 5pm.

"Nope," Jack says, continuing to work on his algebra.

"Well, don't just sit there, go answer it," Mom says.

Sighing deeply, Jack jumps up and shuffles to the door. Peering through the peephole, he sees that there's no one on the front porch. He swings the door open and takes a good look around, but whoever rang the bell has vanished.

"Who was it?" Mom asks.

"A doorbell ghost," Jack says, laughing.

The next afternoon, at 5pm, the doorbell rings two times again. Jack bolts out of his chair, hoping to catch the prankster in the act. But when he flings open the door, again, there's no one there.

It happens the next day, and the next, each time at exactly 5pm. But no one is ever there. Dad checks the wiring of the doorbell, but it's working perfectly.

Mom huffs with frustration. "That's it, I'm installing a security camera," she says.

The next evening, after the prankster had been and gone, they gather around the grainy security footage on Mom's laptop. On-screen, a shadowy man swings open their front gate and glides down the garden path to the front door, ringing the doorbell. Jack sees himself on-screen, opening the front door to him. The man was *right* in front of him, but Jack hadn't seen a soul.

"He wasn't there, I swear!" Jack insists, ice running through his veins.

Just then, the doorbell rings again. Twice.

# Aunt Tina's Painting

## SCARE RATING

"Aunt Tina left you something in her will," Mom says.

"Cash?" I ask hopefully.

I never liked Aunt Tina. She confused me with Tomas, the brother she hated, who had stolen the family inheritance and run away to Mexico. She had always said I looked just like him. Sometimes she pinched me on the arm with her long purple nails. Once, she even drew blood.

"It's Aunt Tina's most prized possession," Mom says. "A painting of her from when she was a kid."

Mom hands me a drab painting of a young Aunt Tina with ringlets, a kitten, a puppy, and a parasol. She looks like an old-fashioned doll. A miserable one.

"I *really* don't want it," I insist. The painting gives me the creeps.

"Just hang it down in the basement. Your aunt would like that."

37

Once I've shoved the ugly painting in the basement, I forget all about it. A couple of weeks later I jump down the stairs to grab my skateboard. Glancing at the frame, I do a double-take at the painting. The center of the painting, right where Aunt Tina should be, is empty.

I blink and rub my eyes. I must be imagining it.

I scramble toward the stairs, but stumble over a box and the basement door slams shut above me. As I look back over my shoulder, little Aunt Tina is out of her painting and crawling on her hands and knees toward me.

*Inspired by the true story of the Hands Resist Him haunted painting by William Stoneham.*

# Night Terrors

## SCARE RATING

Penny woke in the middle of the night. She tried to sit up, but she couldn't move—there was a heavy weight on her chest, pinning her down to the bed. It felt like there was something, or *someone* sitting on her chest!

As her eyes adjusted to the
darkness, Penny saw an old
hag was sitting right on
top of her. The bony
hag put her wrinkled,
warty hands around
Penny's neck,
digging her
long black
nails in, deeper
and deeper . . .
Penny struggled
for breath,
terrified. Gasping
for air, and
scratching at the witch's

face, Penny let out a gurgled groan. Her parents raced to the
room, turning on the light.

"What's wrong, Penny?!" asked Dad.

Penny sat up in the sudden light and looked frantically
around the room. With the flick of a switch, the hag was gone.

"There was someone here," Penny said, hot tears running
down her face. "A witch was trying to kill me!"

"There's no one here but us," said Mom. "You must have
been having a bad dream."

Penny looked around the room; *had* it been a dream? She
began to relax. If the hag had been real, how could she have
disappeared so quickly?

But then Mom touched Penny's bruised and tender skin, puzzled.

"Penny, what are these scratches around your neck? Who did this?"

# Will You Play with Me?

## SCARE RATING 💀 💀

I've ridden my bike past the old, dilapidated children's hospital a hundred times but never had the guts to go inside . . . until today.

The building is covered in thick vines, the windows are smashed in, the brick walls are crumbling. People say it's haunted by the patients who died there years ago.

"We have to spend *at least* ten minutes inside," Elias says, holding out his pinkie for me to swear.

"Deal," I say. I wasn't scared.

I shake his finger, take a deep breath, and climb in

through a broken side window, jumping down onto the dusty, rotten floorboards, sending cockroaches skittering.

"You first!" Elias says, as we walk up the stairs, past rusty steel hospital beds and odd piles of pans.

I stop in my tracks halfway up the stairs and listen; squeaky wheels roll along the floor above us.

"Did you hear that?" I whisper, heart in my mouth. "There it is again!"

Elias drops the tough guy act and grips my arm.

"Let's get out of here!" he says.

"We can't, ten minutes remember?" I say, swallowing my fear.

I force one foot in front of the other, climbing the stairs higher into the building.

There is a figure in a wheelchair at the top of the stairs; a pale-faced boy wearing striped pajamas, a ball in his hand.

"Will you play with me?" he asks, dropping the ball down the stairs toward us.

I pick up the ball and look up to the landing again, but the boy is gone.

Ghost hunters or paranormal investigators stake out haunted places and attempt to collect evidence of ghostly activity using modern gadgets like EMF meters, digital thermometers, video cameras (including thermographic and night vision cameras), and digital audio recorders. The resulting ghostly evidence is often really scary!

# Baby Monitor

## SCARE RATING

While her mom runs errands in town, Eva works on an essay for school, glancing at the baby monitor every now and again to make sure her two-year-old sister, Celeste, is still napping.

Eva smiles when she hears her Mom's voice gently singing to Celeste and sees her shadow on the monitor, bending over the crib. *Guess I didn't notice her get home*, Eva thinks to herself.

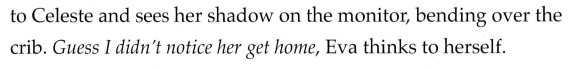

"Go to sleep . . . go to sleep . . ." her mom says to Celeste.

Celeste giggles as Mom keeps singing the lullaby. *Good luck getting her back to sleep*, Eva thinks as she snaps her laptop shut and goes to join them. Walking down the hall, she hears the front door slam. Shocked, she rushes out to see Mom arriving home with bags of groceries.

"Did you come home earlier?" Eva asks, panicking.

"Of course not. I just got back. How's Celeste?" Mom asks. "Still asleep?"

Eva's body floods with fear as she rushes down the hall and flings open the nursery door to find Celeste lying in her crib, still giggling. Eva searches the room, opening the wardrobe and checking under the crib, but there's no one there.

"Eva, what's wrong?" Mom says, watching with concern as her daughter frantically scours the room. "You look like you've seen a ghost."

"Mama! Look!" Celeste says, pointing to where the shadow had only moments before been bending over the crib. "Lady sing to me."

# Come Inside the House

## SCARE RATING

I sip my sweet tea, just like my grandma used to make it, rocking in her favorite chair on her porch . . . the one she was sitting in when she had her heart attack three years ago, and died.

"Come inside the house, Gia," Grandma's voice calls from the kitchen.

I pause, mid-rock. It can't possibly be her; I'm hearing voices in my head. I keep rocking, looking out to her prized rose garden, thinking about how much I miss her and wishing she was really here.

"*Gia! Come inside the house*," says my grandma's voice again, louder and more insistent this time.

I stop rocking entirely; the voice sounds so real.

"Gia, get in the house now!"

I leap out of the chair and do what she says.

Ghosts & Ghouls

As soon as I make it inside the doorway, I hear a deafening crash behind me. A heavy, cast-iron light fixture has fallen from the roof right on top of the chair I was sitting on, breaking it into pieces.

A shiver runs down my spine.

"Thank you," I say out loud, hoping Grandma can hear. "Thank you, Grandma."

## SCARY BUT TRUE!

Not all ghosts are scary. Marie Laveau, a Voodoo Queen who died in 1881, is thought to grant wishes. Believers visit the Voodoo Tomb in New Orleans and leave cash, food, or flowers at her grave.

# Haunted Rocking Horse

## SCARE RATING 💀 💀 💀

It's past midnight in my Great-Aunt Sara's house. Looking after her home while she is away, I have to sleep in the creepy loft room stuffed with antique toys, mildewed books, and chests filled with ancient, yellowed newspapers. Wide awake, I jump at

every little sound. I pull the quilt cover closer to my chin and shiver.

Across the room, there's a slow, rhythmic creaking sound. The rocking gets louder and faster. I peek over to the other side of the room where the toys are, and see the old hobby horse rocking back and forth . . . all on its own.

As the horse starts rocking its way across the room toward me I bury my head under the blankets, breathing hard, my heart racing. It's right next to the bed, *rock, rock, rock*.

The covers tightly around me, I wait it out, too petrified to look out from under the covers. Eventually, the horse stops rocking and I fall into a restless sleep.

In the morning, the hobby horse is back in its usual spot by the toy chest. Nothing seems out of the ordinary and I wonder if I had a terrible nightmare.

In the dining room, Mom greets me with a plate of pancakes and ruffles my hair.

"Can you please not play with Great-Aunt Sara's toys after bedtime?" she asks as she sets my plate in front of me. "We could hear you rocking on Michael's old hobby horse in the middle of the night."

It hadn't been a dream. "Michael?" I say. "Who's Michael?"

"You would have had a great-uncle, but the poor boy died of pneumonia when he was six, here in this very house."

I open my mouth to speak but no words come out.

# I Saw You

## SCARE RATING

"I'm going on my tablet, Mom!" Nia shouts as she clambers up the stairs to her room.

"Homework, first!" Mom shouts back.

"*This is* homework—I'm looking up historic places on internet maps."

Nia grabs her tablet and searches for the Tower of London, once an infamous prison, which she's been studying in history class. With two fingers, she zooms closer and closer into the image of the building until she feels like she's really there!

She taps on an old stone building—the Traitor's Gate, through which prisoners were dragged to the torture chambers. A chill runs down Nia's arms as she notices a figure on the screen, lugging a heavy sack and leaving behind a thick red trail. He's wearing an executioner's hood.

The man in the still image suddenly looks up and Nia feels like he's seen her. But that's impossible! With a sharp breath, she shuts down the app and runs into the kitchen.

"Finished already?" asks Mom.

"Yeah, all done," says Nia, still spooked.

Later, Nia opens the app again, searching in her own country, the USA—far away from the Tower of London. She taps in a quiet street in her neighborhood, Rockley Road, Pleasantville, zooming in on number 34, a house for sale. Again, she gets the eerie feeling she's being watched. The house looks normal—white picket fence, green manicured lawns—but as she zooms closer, there are bloody handprints on the windows and a message: **I SAW YOU**

Nia quickly clicks off the house and types in her home address, surely *that* won't be weird. She zooms in to her house and freezes in horror. Standing in her front yard, staring into her own bedroom window, is the face of the Traitor's Gate executioner. He pulls his leather hood over his face and walks toward the front door.

# Writing's on the Wall

## SCARE RATING 💀💀

"Juan, you need to shower!" shouts Mom, and she's right, I do smell pretty bad after my soccer game. "We're packing up the house for the movers today, and I need your help."

I drag myself away from the TV to the bathroom, grabbing a towel.

Mom thinks our rental house is haunted by the ghost of a teenage girl who died here—murdered by an intruder. Doors slam at night, cups and plates fly out of the cupboards on their own, and a blood-curdling scream woke me up one night. Ever

since then, I try to avoid being alone in the house. We can't move out soon enough.

As I stand in the shower, quickly soaping up and letting the warm water run over my head, the tap turns all the way to hot. I yelp and jump away from the scalding stream, turning the cold up. My heart beats double-time as I rinse off and open the screen door.

On the mirror, an invisible finger is writing on the steamy surface.

**Don't go. I'm lonely.**

Stunned, I back away from the mirror and into the door handle, reaching behind me to find it's locked from the outside.

# CHAPTER 4
# Creepy Creatures & Critters

# Slinky's Big Meal

## SCARE RATING

Mom bought me a snake for my 10th birthday; a 12-foot python called Slinky. It's the best present ever!

Slinky lives in a tank in my room that I share with my little brother, Leo. Slinky is so friendly I take him out of the tank sometimes and let him slither around the house, or in our back garden. Leo and I like to pet Slinky and even drape him around our necks.

When Slinky stopped eating for three days, Mom told me to call the vet.

"I wouldn't worry," said the vet. "Wild snakes have to survive for a long time without eating. He might be starving himself in preparation for a big meal, or maybe he's bored of the food you're giving him."

That evening, I tried giving Slinky new snacks, but he still wouldn't eat.

Late that night, I woke up to a strange rustling in my bed. Slinky was lying beside

me, stretched out straight! I laughed and took him back to his tank.

"You're not a human, Slinky," I reminded him.

The next day, I found him lying beside Leo on the grass, stiff as a board.

I called the vet back.

"Slinky still isn't eating," I said, watching out the window as Leo stood in the back garden with Slinky and our cat. "And there's something else," I said. "He's been doing this weird thing, lying in a straight line all stretched out straight next to me and my brother."

The vet went silent. "Son, that's how snakes measure out their next meal. They lie down next to their prey, sizing them up for eating!"

I looked out the window, just as Slinky rose up, mouth wide, and closed it around Leo's head.

# Never Lick an Envelope

## SCARE RATING

"Do I have to stuff *all* of these?" I ask Mom, as she dumps a huge stack of envelopes and Christmas cards in front of me. She likes to send our boring family-holiday letter out to every distant relative and old friend, so this would take ages.

"Yes, I have to take your brother to soccer practice and these need to be in the post today, thanks Aaron!" she says, rushing out the door.

I lick the first envelope, the glue leaving a gross taste on my tongue. By the time I get to the 100th envelope, my tongue is as dry as the paper.

The next day, my tongue is swollen and throbbing. I look at it in the mirror and there's a strange lump on the tip, too. I can't even eat my breakfast. A week after that, the lump has turned into a huge, fluid-filled blister, and my whole face is swollen up and covered in a strange rash. It's really hard to eat. I feel dizzy and sick.

Mom takes me to the doctor, who pokes and prods at the lump on my tongue until I'm crying in pain, tears running down my blotchy face.

"I have no idea what this is," he says. "We'll have to take an MRI scan."

After the procedure, the doctor squints at the image of my tongue on the screen, puzzled.

"Hmm," he says, squinting, "that looks very much like . . ."

"A cockroach!" I lisp, gripping the sides of the table.

"Perhaps you somehow got cockroach eggs on your tongue . . . Been licking anything unusual lately?"

Dad and I stare at each other in horror. The envelopes must have had cockroach eggs in the glue!

Just then, the skin on my tongue bursts open and I feel the scratch of insect legs crawling out from my lips.

## SCARY BUT TRUE!

When traveling around Southeast Asia, British backpacker Daniela Liverani started suffering from nosebleeds. Back home, she noticed a dark shape wiggling in her nose and she rushed to the emergency department. Doctors discovered Daniela had a 3 in (7.5 cm) leech that had been living up her nose for a month!

# The Elevator Murder

## SCARE RATING

Dina waited for the rickety apartment building elevator to take her down to the playground to meet her friends. The lift doors opened with a creak and she screamed in terror. Slumped in a corner of the cramped lift was her neighbor, Igor. Two wounds punctured his neck and his skin was snow white, a look of pure horror frozen on his features. Dina raced back to her apartment to call for help.

When the police arrived, a detective asked Dina, "Did you see anyone unusual around the building?"

Dina shook her head, she hadn't. What she *had* seen, was her neighbor, scared to death.

From then on, Dina refused to use the elevator, instead, she climbed the stairs.

One day, as the sun set after a long day running around in the playground, with tired legs and a shaking finger, she pressed the elevator call button. The doors opened and there was no one inside. She told herself not to be silly. It was just an elevator.

She pressed her floor—13—and the lift started to move upward. Then, it shuddered to a stop, almost knocking Dina off her feet. The lights blinked out, plunging the elevator into blackness.

There was a long silence and then she heard a loud thumping sound above her. Something was trying to get inside!

"Help!" cried Dina.

She remembered her phone in her pocket and with trembling hands, shone a light in front of her.

Eight huge, shining eyes stared back at her, then a giant spider shot a sticky web of woven silk toward her, lassoing her arms to her sides and gluing her mouth shut so she couldn't even scream.

# Miguel's New Puppy

## SCARE RATING 💀 💀 💀

Miguel and his parents were walking around a street market downtown when he felt a wet snout nuzzling the back of his leg. A small dog with stumpy legs and a long tail was following him.

"Look, Mom, a stray puppy!" he said.

Mom screwed up her face in disgust. "Shoo!" Mom swatted at the animal. "I've never seen such an ugly mutt, must be one of those Mexican hairless dogs."

Miguel dropped behind his parents and scooped up the dog, hiding it in his coat on the drive home. The dog needed a home and Miguel desperately wanted a puppy. This was perfect! Back home, Miguel gave the dog some food and water, brushed its short, matted fur, and made a bed for it out of some old towels, right next to his.

When he woke up, the dog was staring at him with red, watery eyes, a strange white foam dribbling out of its mouth.

"Aw, you've caught a bad cold," Miguel said.

His older brother Carlos burst in and caught him patting the dog. "I knew you were up to something!" Carlos said.

"Don't tell Mom," Miguel begged.

"Where did you get him?" Carlos asked Miguel.

"At the street market in the city. Do you think he's a Mexican hairless dog?"

"This ain't no dog, little brother," Carlos said, shifting nervously from foot to foot. "That's a sewer rat . . . and I think he has rabies."

Miguel snatched at the snarling rat, but it was too late. He watched on in horror as it pounced on Carlos's bare leg and clamped down hard with foaming, razor-sharp teeth.

**SCARY BUT TRUE!**

Just like Alfred Hitchcock's classic horror movie, *The Birds*, in 2013 millions of blackbirds and European starlings invaded a small town in Kentucky, blacking out the sky, terrifying residents, and leaving behind disease-filled droppings.

# La Lechuza's Attack

## SCARE RATING 💀 💀 💀 💀

"Bye, Mom!" I shout as I race down the hall to catch the school bus.

Closing the front door behind me, I notice deep scratches in the wood. What kind of beast would make those?!

Mom follows me outside and clutches my arm in a panic. "These are the claw marks of La Lechuza!" she cries. "She's sent us a warning!"

I roll my eyes. Mom's convinced the cranky old woman who lives down the street is a witch in disguise and at night she turns into a black owl and steals children from their beds.

"Come on, Mom. The Lechuza isn't real," I say. "It's just an old wives' tale."

At dusk, Mom locks all the doors and windows.

"Do *not* leave your bed tonight," she instructs. "No matter what."

I sigh, kiss her goodnight, and do what she says.

Or plan to, anyway.

Late that night, I wake up to the wailing cry of a baby outside my window. It sounds hungry and afraid. Despite Mom's warning, I climb out of bed to investigate, my heart pounding as I creep through the dark house to the front door. But as I step outside to look for the baby, a huge black owl swoops down and seizes me by my shoulders with sharp talons.

It lifts me into the air and I scream in terror. A gunshot cracks from below and the bird drops me to the ground with a thump, winded. Mom holds a hunting rifle, aiming at the owl to shoot again.

The bird flaps unsteadily, injured, blood dripping onto the grass and the path as it flies away.

In the morning, both of us spooked, Mom walks me to the bus, her eyes on the old woman's house.

The door opens, and the elderly lady walks stiffly out to her porch, glaring at my mother. She hobbles on a crutch, her leg bandaged and bloody.

# A Dreadly Tale

## SCARE RATING 💀💀💀

As Caleb grabbed his skateboard on his way to the half-pipe, Mom blocked his way, holding out a comb.

"Comb your hair!" she shouted. "We have guests arriving later."

"No way!" he shouted back, scratching his scalp. He looked after his thick, rolled dreads with a special natural oil, and piled them up on his head in a big bun, but he would never brush them out . . . even if his head *had* been a bit itchy lately.

At the skate park, Caleb dropped into the pipe, losing his balance and smacking his head on the concrete. Bleeding, he called home. His mom drove him to the emergency room immediately.

"I'm sorry, Caleb, but we're going to have to shave off your hair," said the doctor. "You need at least 20 stiches on the back on your skull."

Caleb sulked, but his mom couldn't keep the grin off her face.

As the doctor started shaving off Caleb's matted hair, a black widow spider with long, spindly legs crawled out of Caleb's hair and up the doctor's arm. The doctor dropped the razor, swatting at the deadly creature.

Then more spiders crawled out of Caleb's hair, until every surface in the surgery wriggled and writhed, spiders crawling up the walls and across the sterilized instruments. The nurses ran from the room, screaming.

Caleb reached into his dreadlocks, pulling out thousands of tiny white spider eggs, that had hatched.

# Creature of the Deep
## SCARE RATING 💀 💀 💀 💀

"Race you!" I shout, digging my paddle into the water and heading beyond the breaking waves on my kayak, out to the deeper water.

My older brother, Dave, glides past. He's a much stronger paddler than I am. Better than me at everything, really.

"Come on, Kevin, let's go out further," Dave shouts, leaving me behind.

The lifeguard's tower is a speck on the shore, way back to the left, further away than I expected. We're drifting down the beach in a powerful current.

"Dave! Wait! We're too far out!" I call.

My pulse quickens as a fin slices through the water in the distance. It's probably just a dolphin. There are hundreds out here. Still, I'd like to go in; it's getting late and looks like it might rain.

I feel my kayak jerk to one side, and I'm tipped out into the freezing water.

"Very funny Da—"

My mouth fills with water as I'm yanked straight down to the murky ocean floor. Like a rag doll, I'm thrashed violently side-to-side, a sharp pain shooting up my arm from where whatever it is has a hold of me. I twist around in the water and my blood runs cold. It's a massive great white shark—at least sixteen feet long! Bubbles rush from my mouth as I scream and struggle, trying to poke at the shark's beady black eyes.

It drags me upward. Breaking the surface, I take desperate, ragged breaths.

"Help!" I gurgle.

Above me, Dave's paddle hits the shark on the head, hard. As it briefly unclamps its razor-sharp teeth, Dave grabs my hand and hauls me into his kayak.

He paddles hard for the shore.

I breathe hard, half-sobbing, too afraid to look at my arm, to see what's left of it. I squeeze my eyes closed, count to three, and look.

My hand is still there, wrapped around my paddle with a white-knuckled grip. My paddle, however, has a big, jagged bite mark.

# The Spider Bite

## SCARE RATING

Yuka walked into the cave, shining her torch into the darkness. A colony of bats spread their wings and flapped through the cramped space all around her and over her head. She loved exploring new places—the creepier the better.

As she entered the cave, she walked smack into a sticky cobweb, feeling a hairy spider drop onto her head. She screamed, her voice echoing off the closed-in walls. Spiders were her biggest fear!

She jumped up and down, desperately trying to brush it off. She felt a sharp sting as fangs sank deep into her cheek.

She screamed again, slapping at her face, and sprinted out of the cave, her cheek throbbing.

Back home, the spider bite swelled into an angry, red, round boil, growing bigger and bigger each day. Yuka stood at her bathroom mirror, staring at the aching puss-filled mound. It was huge!

As she stared miserably at the lump, she noticed the bite started to move. Something inside pushed against her skin, trying to get out!

The bite burst open and hundreds of tiny spiders exploded from her, crawling all over her face. Yuka screamed and hit and swatted and tried to get them off her skin, but the tiny spiders all bit at once, puncturing her skin over and over and over.

# Bat Baby

## SCARE RATING

There's a strange scratching sound in Ling's bedroom, and it's not coming from the game she's playing on her tablet. Looking around, she thinks it must be coming from the window. She turns back to her game, but the scratching gets louder.

"Okay, okay," Ling sighs. She climbs off her bed and shuffles to the window. It's probably her little sister, Mei, trying to scare her.

She opens the window to find a small, black, furry animal with an injured wing. It looks like a bat. It's so cute!

Without telling her parents, she decides to keep the bat. Her little sister Mei swears to keep her secret, and together they make a bed for it and a bandage for its broken wing. After a couple of weeks, the bat is healed and flying around her bedroom!

But then one morning, Ling wakes up to find her pillow has some blood on it. She runs to the mirror, pulls back her hair, and her eyes widen as she finds two small bite marks on her neck.

The bat is sleeping soundly on her bed. Its belly looks rounder than usual.

Full, even.

Morning sun streams in the window, and it burns Ling's skin. She closes the blinds and stays in the dark, all day, refusing to play with Mei.

That night, Ling wakes with a start and sits bolt upright. Her teeth have grown bigger in her mouth, forming two sharp fangs.

She crawls to Mei's room, where her sister is sleeping soundly.

But she won't be for long.

SCARY BUT TRUE!

In 2017, one man died and 40 people were bitten by rabies-carrying vampire bats in the South American country of Brazil. The blood-thirsty bats usually feed on animal blood, but they turned to humans after their natural habitats were destroyed.

# CHAPTER 5
# Bumps in the Night

# Mommy, is that You?

## SCARE RATING

Late one night, I wake up to my mom singing upstairs in her study in the attic. Her rocker creaks back and forth on the floorboards. Groggily, I get out of bed and creep through the hallway, to the foot of the steep attic staircase, her pretty notes now clearer and louder. She's singing an old-fashioned song I've never heard before.

"Mommy?" I call up the stairs.

"Yeesss," she sings back.

Smiling, I climb the stairs to crawl into her lap. Maybe we'll have a midnight hot chocolate together and fall asleep by the heater. As I reach for the handle to let myself into the room, I hear the shuffle of footsteps from the hallway.

Mom's slippers!

"Sweetie, why are you up so late?" Mom calls out from the hallway below me.

Startled, I jump away from the attic door and run back down the stairs, burying my face into Mom's robe.

I look back at the staircase. The door opens a crack and a thin, deathly white hand slides out.

I'm staring at an old woman I've never seen before.

## SCARY BUT TRUE!

In almost all cultures, there are stories and legends warning of the dangers of the dark. In fact, the Saxons called night-time the "death mist". Creepy!

# At First, it's Quiet, then they Come

## SCARE RATING

At bedtime, Dimitri grizzles and grumbles, "I'm not tired!" as he grips his mom's arm tightly.

Mom sighs and strokes Dimitri's head, worried by the dark circles around his eyes. He'd been plagued by nightmares since they'd moved to their new house.

"Dimitri, we go through this every night. You need to sleep."

"But the monsters come out when it's dark. Please, *please* leave the light on."

"There's no such thing as monsters," Mom says.

"There is!"

Mom tucks him into bed and flicks off the lights.

"Sweet dreams," she says, closing the door. "I'll be right outside if you need me."

Dimitri pulls his knees to his chest, blinking in the darkness. At first, it's quiet.

Then they come.

Heavy breathing, claws dragging along the carpet. The monster under his bed pushes up hard on his mattress, nearly tipping him off. Dimitri whimpers as they prowl his room, throwing his things around.

"Go away! You're not real," Dimitri whispers.

The wardrobe door opens slowly, and Dimitri sees the shadow of the scariest one, gnashing its sharp teeth, green eyes glowing in the dark. Moving closer, closer . . .

Dimitri screams and Mom rushes into the room, filling

the room with light. Her shocked eyes dart around. Every toy has been tipped out, and the carpet is ripped.

"Dimitri! Did you do this?"

"No, Mom, the monsters did it, "Dimitri says, quivering in fear.

"I don't want to tell you again," says Mom. "Monsters aren't real."

Dimitri nods as the end of a scaly, slimy tail flicks back under the bed, and emerald eyes retreat into the wardrobe.

# The Midnight Game

## SCARE RATING 💀💀💀💀

"Wake up, Jimmy!" my sister Simone whispers, prodding me awake. "It's time."

I rub my eyes, still half asleep. We're going to play The Midnight Game; everyone at school is talking about it. We write our names on a piece of paper and add a pinprick of our blood. We creep toward the front door, careful not to wake our parents. After placing the paper at the front door, Simone lights a candle.

"Now?" I whisper.

"Not yet," says Simone, watching the clock.

As the clock strikes midnight, she gives me a nod and I take a deep, nervous breath and knock softly on the door 22 times. Simone opens the front door and blows out the candle. Then she closes the door and relights the candle. According to the rules of the game, the small flickering light is our protection against the evil spirit. Now we had to survive the night.

"Oh my gosh," she whispers with a nervous laugh, "we just invited the Midnight Man into our house." Simone's eyes are wide with fear.

We creep around the house in the dark for a while, peering at flickering shadows on the walls for movement, then huddle behind the sofa in the living room, holding the candle between us. The house is quiet and there's no sign of the mysterious Midnight Man. My head drops onto Simone's shoulder.

"Do *not* fall asleep, Jimmy!" says Simone. "He'll get you."

All of a sudden, in the still air, our candle blows out. Simone's eyes widen in terror.

"He's here," she whispers.

The room turns icy cold as Simone fumbles to relight the candle. I pour a shaky circle of salt around us—our last line of defense against the Midnight Man. *Why did we play this game?*

The front door opens with a long, loud creak, and I peek around the sofa.

There, towering above us, is the shadowy figure of the Midnight Man.

*Based on the ancient pagan ritual-turned scary sleepover game,* The Midnight Game.

# Buckets of Fun

## SCARE RATING 💀💀💀

"That'll be $2," Jeremy says, and I hand over the money.

Every year my friend Jeremy runs the Scary Feel Boxes stand at my school's Halloween Night Fair, creating boxes of gloopy, disgusting gunk that you put your hand in to feel.

"Watch out for the zombie brains!" he says cheerfully as I push my way through the tent flaps and into the darkened space.

The first box is labeled **VEINS AND WORMS.** I reach in tentatively, my fingers squishing into a mess of slippery strands . . . I'm guessing it's cooked spaghetti!

Next is **EYEBALLS.** I pull a handful of peeled grapes out of the box. Nice one, Jeremy.

I move along to **HEARTS**, and squelch something round and soft. Boiled tomatoes. Eeeww!

The mystery boxes get even more disgusting— **ZOMBIE BRAINS** are actually soaked, soapy sponge; **ROTTING MAGGOTS & BUGS** are rice and raisins.

The last box is simply labeled **SURPRISE.**

*Strange.*

I wiggle my fingers around in the box. There's nothing in there. It's a trick box. Just air.

A hand grabs mine inside the box and pulls hard, my arm sliding into the box to my armpit. I struggle to escape the vise-like grip, eventually twisting my hand free.

I run out of the tent, rubbing the red welts on my wrist.

"Jeremy, that was the best trick ever!" I say, once my heart has stopped racing.

"What are you talking about?" Jeremy asks, puzzled.

"The hand in the box?" I say. "So scary! Who was it?"

Jeremy shakes his head, confused.

"What hand?"

## SCARY BUT TRUE!

According to scientific studies, humans are more likely to cheat or act dishonestly when they're in a dim room, rather than a brightly lit one! So, if your sibling has borrowed your stuff, make sure to ask them about it with the lights on!

# Dancing in the Moonlight
## SCARE RATING

"Go straight home, don't talk to strangers," says Derek, letting out a dramatic cackle as he shuts the door in Stan's face.

After a late night watching scary movies with his friends, Stan feels jumpy walking down the quiet street toward his house. It's pitch black out and he opens the flashlight app on his phone, shining it ahead. On the other side of the street a man walks toward him. Stan squints as he comes closer. Wait he's . . . dancing?

The tall, thin man waltzes gracefully toward Stan. He's wearing a wrinkled, faded tuxedo with tails at the back. The man crosses over the street to the same side as Stan, and his face is briefly illuminated by the streetlight.

Stan stiffens. The man's head is tilted toward the night sky, eyes wide open, an unnatural, cartoonish smile of pure bliss on his face.

Stan picks up the pace, running quickly across the street, trying to lose the dancing man. He looks behind him and relaxes. The man has vanished.

Eyes back on the ground in front, Stan stops in his tracks. The dancing man is crouching in a hedge up ahead. *How did he get there so fast?*

As their eyes lock, the man leaps out of the bushes, sprinting toward Stan at full speed, a goofy, ghoulish grin still on his face.

*Based on the urban legend of The Smiling Man.*

# What Happened in the Dark

## SCARE RATING 💀💀💀💀

"Are we there yet?" I moan, as my mom drives down an unfamiliar narrow road, high beams illuminating the darkness ahead.

We're on our way home after a trip to my grandma's house. She lives in the countryside, hundreds of miles from the city. Mom grips the wheel tighter, stressed.

"I took a wrong turn somewhere."

79

She slows the car in front of a stone tunnel.

"We're officially lost," she sighs in frustration. "And we have no signal out here, so I can't use the GPS."

The road is too narrow to turn, so Mom drives slowly into the black tunnel. As we do, our headlights flicker out, and there's a loud bang on the rear bumper. I twist around but no cars are behind us. What just hit us? We're alone in the tunnel.

*Bang! Bang! Bang!*

All around us something in the dark is hitting the car, again and again and again, shaking us in our seats.

After a few moments the headlights come back on weakly and Mom presses her foot on the accelerator. After what feels like forever, we exit the tunnel and drive into a nearby gas station.

We leap out of the car and hug each other tightly, our hearts racing.

My blood runs cold as I see the handprints. They're all over the windows, covering every last inch of glass.

After a few attempts at cleaning, I drop the squeegee back in the bucket of soapy water.

"I can't get the prints off," I say to Mom. "They're on the *inside* of the car."

**SCARY BUT TRUE!**

Nyctophobia is a severe fear of the dark. It's triggered by the brain's perception of the scary things that *could* happen in a dark environment.

# The Face at the Window

## SCARE RATING

Home alone with her younger brother Felix, Clara watched TV. She wanted to wait up for her parents to come home, even though it was late and she was sleepy.

She turned her attention to the sliding glass doors behind by the TV to watch the snow fall outside.

But that's not what she saw.

Clara let out a piercing scream; a hooded man was staring at her through the thick glass.

A knife glinted in his hand.

Clara scrambled for the phone and called the police, and then her parents. When the police arrived, they looked for footprints outside in the newly-fallen snow. But there were none outside the sliding door.

"But he was right there!" Clara insisted.

Puzzled, the police entered the house and found wet footprints leading from the side laundry door, to the couch where Clara had been sitting.

Clara's dad hugged her tightly as he and the policemen shared a nervous glance.

"Clara, you're a very lucky girl," one of the officers said.

"How come?" she asked.

After her scary night, she didn't *feel* very lucky.

"The man staring at you wasn't standing outside in the snow," the policeman said. He gestured to the rug below them

where a pair of wet footprints was starting to dry. "He was standing behind the couch. Right behind *you*! What you saw was his reflection in the glass."

*Based on the popular urban legend,* The Killer's Reflection.

# Sleepwalking Spirit

## SCARE RATING 💀 💀 💀

"Don't wake up, don't wake up," the girl's voice sings softly.

Taking her small, pale hand, I swing my legs out of my warm bed at the mountain cabin we're vacationing in and follow her sweet voice down the dark hallway, like I'm in a trance.

"It's this way, don't be afraid," the girl whispers as she opens the front door and we step outside into the icy night. Without even grabbing my jacket or snow shoes, I walk down the path. The frozen path stings my feet, but it's like the pain is far away, through a haze, perhaps happening to someone else.

"Keep up!" the girl shouts, she pulls me through the woods. It's misty, and I can hardly make out the trees all around me. *Where am I?*

"Down here! I'm waiting!" the girl shouts from somewhere below.

Tired, I stop to take a breath. As I do, the mist clears from around my feet.

My toes are just over the edge of a deep ravine.

I can't move, I can't even breathe; if I move even an inch I'll tumble hundreds of feet onto the sharp rocks below.

A hand grabs my shoulder and hauls me back from the edge.

"Sweetie, what are you doing out here?!" says my dad. "Have you been sleepwalking?"

As he wraps a jacket around my shoulders and walks me back to the house, I hear the girl's voice echoing in the ravine.

"Don't go to sleep," she says. "I'll be waiting . . ."

## SCARY BUT TRUE!

'Night terror' is a sleep disorder that causes people to wake up screaming, wide-eyed in, well, terror! It usually occurs in the first hours of lighter, non-rapid eye movement (NREM) sleep.

# CHAPTER 6
# Terrifying Toys & Sinister Clowns

# End of the Road

## SCARE RATING

After her late shift at the diner, Skyler's mom picked him up from his friend's place and they drove home via an abandoned road out of town. It was close to midnight, and Skyler was half-asleep, drool on his chin. He woke with a start when his mom hit the brakes, tires squealing on the wet tar. "What in the world?" Mom murmured.

There were at least 100 toy clowns arranged in a neat row along the road's divider. Each one had a painted white face, a red ball nose, and baggy, colorful outfit. The dolls' black eyes shined in the headlights. Mom opened the door slowly. "I'll take a quick look."

"Don't!" Skyler whispered, grabbing her arm. "It might be a trap! I'll come with you."

He got out of the car, heart hammering, and walked toward the toys behind his mom. Why would anyone leave so many clown dolls out in the rain? He bent down to pick one up, turning the strange doll over and pulling on a cord at its back. The doll broke into an evil, plastic laugh, turned its head to Skyler and gripped his arm tightly with plastic fingers.

"Don't be scared. We just want someone to play with us."

The toy clowns formed a tight circle around them, moving closer . . . closer . . . a chorus of evil laughs filling the silence.

*Based on the* Camanche Road Mystery.

**SCARY BUT TRUE!**

A fear of clowns is called coulrophobia and just the sight of a red nose can leave some people quaking in fear. Scientists say it's because of the "uncanny valley" effect, in which humans feel revulsion or fear at an image that looks "almost human".

# No Returns

## SCARE RATING

The Pixie rag doll was on sale for $7.99 and Scarlett *had* to have it. She adored its button eyes and crooked, stitched lips.

"Mom! Can I buy a doll online?" she shouted. When she heard nothing in reply, she pressed the "buy" button.

Soon enough, the doll arrived and Scarlett ripped open the box, hugging the doll to her chest.

"Pixie! You're finally here!" she cried.

That night, Scarlett laid the doll next to her in bed and fell fast asleep. In the morning, she was shocked to find scratches on her cheeks . . . and her new doll's cotton hands streaked with blood.

*Her* blood.

Scarlett decided to put the doll in her toy cupboard that night—shutting the door firmly. But the next morning, the doll was lying next to her in bed, button eyes seeming to stare at her accusingly. Scarlett flung the doll across the room. She spun around angrily and froze when she caught sight of herself in the mirror. Her arms and legs were covered in scratches.

Scarlett screamed.

"What happened? What's wrong?!" her mom cried, running into the room.

After Scarlett told her mom about the doll, they took it to the garden and buried it.

"Good riddance," Mom said, tipping in the last shovelful of dirt.

Scarlett left for school the following day, tripping on something on the doorstep. She picked it up, her whole body shaking in fear. It was the rag doll, covered in dirt.

"I'm sending it back," said Mom angrily, taking it to the post office.

A week later they got a call from the seller.

"A package arrived from you," the woman said. "But the box was empty. Is Pixie up to her old tricks?"

# Molly the Dolly

## SCARE RATING 💀💀💀

"Please, Mommy? *Please* can I have her?"

Yi Mei pointed at a porcelain doll in a glass display box. It looked like a real girl, with curly brown hair, a downturned mouth, and long, curled eyelashes. The doll was holding up five fingers.

"How much?" her mom asked the shop assistant.

"Not for sale," she said firmly.

Yi Mei pouted and stamped her foot.

"Everything is for sale," said Mom. "One hundred dollars?"

The shop assistant shook her head.

"Two hundred?" asked Mom. "It's my daughter's birthday present."

Reluctantly, the shop assistant unlocked the display case and took the doll off the shelf.

"Don't leave your daughter alone with this doll," she said, wrapping it up.

"Don't be silly," said Yi Mei, hugging the doll. "We're going to be best friends!"

At home, Yi Mei played with her new doll all afternoon, but left it on the staircase after dinner.

"Pick up your doll," said Mom.

"Sure," promised Yi Mei. "Later."

But she forgot all about the doll and went to bed without her.

Later, she woke up to hear a soft voice calling for her.

"Yi Mei! Yi Mei! Come get me!"

Yi Mei climbed out of bed and to the top of the stairs, but her doll wasn't on the step where she had left it.

A child's voice whispered in her ear. "I'm behind you."

Yi Mei felt two small hands push at her legs, and she tumbled down the stairs, feeling her leg snap. Her mother found her at the bottom of the stairs, crying in pain.

Yi Mei picked up the doll and noticed that its lips were now curled into a smile.

It was holding up two hands with six fingers.

*Based on the urban legend* Six Fingers *or* The Molly Dolly.

**SCARY BUT TRUE!**

The haunted Raggedy Ann doll that inspired the 2014 horror movie, *Annabelle*, now lies in glass box in The Warrens' Occult Museum in Monroe, Connecticut. The museum's owners—Ed and Lorraine Warren—say the doll is possessed by a dead girl's spirit.

# Black Balloon

## SCARE RATING 💀 💀 💀 💀

It was all over the news: a creepy clown was roaming the city, lurking in parks and on street corners.

Sean's school had sent out a letter to all parents, warning that kids should stay away from anyone dressed as a clown.

After class, Sean went to shoot hoops at the school's basketball courts. He grinned as the ball swished through the net; with all the fuss about clown sightings, he had the courts to himself. He nailed a perfect three-pointer when he heard a slow clap from across the court.

A clown watched him from the sideline, holding a black balloon. His costume was gray and tattered and he had a sinister, black-painted smile on his face.

Sean's pulse quickened and he wiped sweat from his brow.

He was stupid to have been so careless about being out by himself after school.

The clown walked slowly toward him, holding out the balloon. Sean grabbed his bike and took off down the street.

As he neared home, Sean saw the clown sitting alone at a bus stop, making a sad face and waving at him with the tips of his fingers. Sean pedaled as fast as he could. As he raced through the back streets, he checked anxiously behind him; luckily, the clown wasn't following him.

Throwing his bike down on his front lawn, Sean sprinted to his front door, stopping in his tracks halfway down the path.

Tied to the front door handle was a single black balloon.

As he moved closer to his house, Sean stopped. He didn't know what to do. On the doormat were two oversized red clown shoes.

# The Clown Mask

## SCARE RATING

Luis's uncle had recently passed away, and his family had inherited his run-down house. "My uncle used to manage a circus," my friend Luis said as he led me through the front door.

"You want to check out the attic? There's loads of weird stuff up there."

"Sure, I guess," I said.

Luis opened the pull-down stairs and we climbed up into the musty attic space. It was stuffed full of circus costumes and props. I lifted up a fake barbell made of polystyrene with just one finger.

"Check me out, I'm the strong man!" I joked.

Luis took out two wooden juggling pins and threw them in the air. They hit the floor in a loud clatter that made me jump.

"Let's go now," I said, getting an uneasy feeling about rifling through his uncle's possessions.

"Wait! Look at this!" Luis said, grabbing a clown mask from a box. The mask had white, wrinkled skin, a crooked grin, and limp blue hair.

"Put that back," I said. "It's giving me the heebie-jeebies."

"Relax, Ramon," Luis said. "It's just a bunch of circus junk."

Luis slipped the clown mask over his face and started dancing, letting out a long, evil laugh. At first, I chuckled but then Luis started spinning around the room, faster and faster.

He clawed at the mask, his body writhing, like he couldn't stop. Then he collapsed on the floor, completely still.

I rushed over to him and ripped the mask from his face.

Luis lay there, still, staring at the ceiling. His face was plastered with thick white stage makeup, and his nose had turned bulbous and red. His mouth was twisted into a grimace and then he let out a long giggle, took the clown mask from my hands, and slipped it over my face.

# Island of the Dolls

## SCARE RATING 💀💀💀💀

Maria stops walking, her mouth dropping open in shock.

The *Island of the Dolls* tour had wandered through the woods to a tree strung up with hundreds of old, weathered dolls. The dolls swing from low-hanging branches, lifeless eyes staring at nothing. Some dolls are beheaded, some missing limbs and eyes; their dresses tatty and dirty.

Maria shivers as the cold, glass gaze of a doll finds hers.

"My uncle was a caretaker on this island," says the guide. "When he arrived, he found a young girl had drowned in the canal with her doll floating nearby.

To settle the girl's restless spirit, he hung dolls from these trees for her to play with . . . for 50 years he hung more and more dolls for her . . . until his body was also found in the canal."

The other tourists take lots of photos, but tears spring to Maria's eyes.

"The dolls look so lonely," she whispers to her mom. "They need someone to care for them."

"They're creepy; leave them alone," warns Mom.

"You don't want to take one of these, young lady," the tour guide says. "Rumor has it they're haunted."

But Maria doesn't believe him. Dolls don't belong on trees on deserted islands; they need little girls to play with them.

As the tour moves on, a chorus of giggles and whispers echo from the tree. Maria unties a baby doll with pink cheeks and brown hair. She slips the doll into her backpack and re-joins the group, squeezing her mom's hand tightly.

Back at their hotel that evening, Maria brushes the doll's hair and washes years of grime off her face. As she climbs into bed, she hears the creak of her bedroom window opening and an icy wind chills the room.

A small girl, soaked and sickly-looking, stands in a puddle of water next to the window. Maria clasps the doll tightly to her chest.

"That's mine," the girl says in a low, threatening whisper. "Give it back."

*Based on the real-life* Island of the Dolls *tourist attraction in Mexico.*

# Blind Faith

## SCARE RATING

Yanjun loved the *Hungry Ghost Festival*, the time of year when spirits and ancestors came back to their homes in Hong Kong to visit the living. He ran down his street on his way to school, careful not to disturb his neighbor's offerings of sweet orange cakes, and burnt piles of paper money. The air smelled like incense and ash.

"Wait for me, Yanjun!" cried his sister, Fen.

Yanjun slowed his pace when he reached a doll tied to a tree. The doll had shiny brown hair and a pink dress, but its eyes were tied with a thick blindfold. Fen reached out and stroked the doll's hair.

"I want to keep her," Fen said.

"We shouldn't take it. It might be a ghost offering," said Yanjun.

Fen's little lip stuck out and she began crying. She didn't have many toys and Yanjun felt sorry for her.

"Please, Yanjun," she said. "*Please, please, please?*"

Yanjun sighed as he untied the doll for his sister.

"Okay, but don't tell anyone where you got it."

Fen cradled the doll and a letter fell out of the blindfold.

## WARNING! THIS DOLL IS POSSESSED BY AN EVIL SPIRIT. I BOUND HER EYES SO SHE WOULDN'T FOLLOW ME HOME. IF YOU REMOVE THE BLINDFOLD, YOU WILL BE CURSED.

Yanjun's body filled with fear. "Fen! Wait!"

He tried to snatch the doll from Fen's arms, but she had already removed the blindfold and was staring into the doll's cold eyes, mesmerized.

Fen blinked. She blinked again, swaying on her feet. "I don't feel so good," she whispered. She dropped the doll and crumpled in a heap on the ground.

## SCARY BUT TRUE!

Disneyland cast members claim that the dolls in the "It's A Small World" ride come alive after dark. The ride features over 300 audio-animatronic children from all over the world. Happiest place on earth? Maybe not.

# The Visitor in the Storm

## SCARE RATING

Thunder rumbled outside my bedroom window, making it impossible to get to sleep. Lightning lit up the room and I saw my dad standing in the doorway. It seemed he couldn't sleep, either.

"Dad?" I whispered.

Propping myself up on my elbows to get a better look, I stiffened.

That wasn't my dad.

The figure half-turned; he had a long nose like a carrot and wore a pointed cone hat, ruffled white collar, and red

and yellow jumpsuit. My heart raced as the figure pointed his gloved hand toward me and beckoned with one finger. Ghoulish, fake laughter echoed around the room.

Terrified, I clutched my blankets around me and shuffled back into the corner of the bed, shaking.

The clown put his hand on his belly and mimed laughter, now pointing his finger at the lower bunk, where my brother Oliver was sleeping. He started to creep toward Oliver with long, exaggerated steps. I forced myself to leap off the bunk onto the floor below.

"Wake up, Oliver!" I shouted, dragging him, bleary-eyed, out of bed. The clown blocked the doorway, but I pushed past him, feeling his fingers grab my T-shirt as we escaped.

I burst into my parent's room, breathless.

"There's a clown! In our room! Come quickly!"

Dad flicked the light switch on, but the clown was gone. "You're safe, boys," said Dad. "I've checked and no one has been in the house. The alarm is still on. It was just a bad dream."

He turned off the light, and shut the door firmly. As I drifted off to sleep, I heard the faint giggle of clown's laughter echoing in the wind.

## SCARY BUT TRUE!

A gift from his grandmother in his childhood, Robert Eugene Otto had an antique toy called Robert the Doll which was the inspiration behind the 1988 *movie*, *Child's Play*, which featured a demonic toy called Chucky. Robert is believed to giggle, change facial expressions, and move items around. Freaky!

# Talking Timmy

## SCARE RATING

Alecia adored her Christmas present—Talking Timmy was a doll that could talk, move, and even sing songs! Alecia gave Timmy a big hug and kissed his cheek every night before bed.

Every night, Timmy would say, "I love you," and every night, Alecia would say, "Aw, I love you, too, Timmy!"

But when Alecia brought her friend Zoe home to play, Zoe wasn't impressed by Timmy at all.

"Those dolls are for babies," Zoe said. "I got one three years ago."

"Yeah, I don't like it anymore," Alecia said, turning red.

She threw Timmy roughly into the back of her cupboard, knocking the batteries out of their compartment.

That night, Alecia heard a rustling sound coming from the wardrobe.

"I love you!" said a familiar voice.

Timmy.

Alecia sat up in bed, alarmed. How could the doll still talk? Its batteries were out! Nervously, she climbed out of bed and then slowly opened the wardrobe door. Timmy's eyes lit up in the dark.

"You can't get rid of me that easily," Timmy said in a menacing voice.

Alecia screamed and grabbed Timmy, turning him over and ripping out the wiring to the doll's microphone. Timmy's eyes dulled and he fell silent once more. Alecia locked him in her toy box, keeping the key under her pillow.

"You're going to the garbage dump, Timmy," she said loudly.

In the morning, she woke to find Talking Timmy sitting on her pillow. Terrified, Alecia turned to face Timmy, as his plastic fingers closed like a vise around her arm.

"We're going to be together forever, Alecia," Timmy said in a deep growl.

## SCARY BUT TRUE!

In 2017 in the UK a teenage girl, Tia Mariah McBean, was prosecuted for sending her ex-boyfriend a cursed voodoo doll. Some people believe if you stick pins into a voodoo doll, you can inflict real pain on your enemies.

# Horror Haircut

## SCARE RATING

Mike thought his sister Amy's dolls were stupid. All she did was brush their hair all day and talk to them in a silly voice. She wouldn't even come out and play with him anymore. One afternoon, when Amy was with their mom at the dentist, Mike snuck into Amy's room, picking out her favorite doll with flowing blonde hair and a pink, sparkly ballgown.

Mike took out the pair of scissors he'd swiped from the kitchen and hacked off the doll's long locks until she was bald. He wrote **STUPID** in black marker on the doll's forehead, and tucked the evidence into his pocket.

When Amy came home from the dentist, Mike waited by her bedroom door to see her reaction to her doll's new haircut. But Amy just skipped out of the room happily, holding the doll in her hand. Its hair had grown back to the same long length it was before. Even the pen marks had vanished. He stared at the doll in disbelief; it felt like she was staring right back at him.

"Dolls are stupid," he muttered.

Mike slept with his door closed that night, still thinking about the doll.

In the morning he shuffled sleepily to the bathroom and looked at himself in the mirror, gasping at his own reflection.

His hair had been shaved off and across his forehead in blue ink was scribbled **NOT AS STUPID AS YOU.**

# CHAPTER 7
# Monster Mash

# Bewere the Wolf

## SCARE RATING

Buddy had a big math test coming up and couldn't sleep; he was so worried about it. He tossed and turned in his bed until just before dawn, when he gave up on sleep, got dressed, and crept down to the garden shed to grab his bike for an early morning ride.

As he walked through the dewy grass, he heard a low, threatening growl. Taking a few more tentative steps, Buddy came face-to-face with a shaggy black wolf, its teeth bared, ready to attack him.

He couldn't believe his eyes—*what was a wolf doing in his yard?*

Buddy backed away slowly, his heart hammering in his chest, maintaining eye contact with the animal, like his dad had taught him.

Saliva dripped from its sharp teeth. If he turned and ran, Buddy feared he wouldn't escape.

As Buddy and the wolf stared each other down, the first rays of sun broke over the horizon, casting an orange glow over the yard. The wolf dropped its head and ran into the bushes, whimpering.

Buddy jumped over the fence for cover and nervously peered back over to where the wolf had disappeared.

But instead of a wolf, there was a man crawling out of the bushes where the wolf had hidden. In the dawn light, the stark-naked man scurried away. He grabbed a sheet from the washing line and took off, jumping fences and disappearing from sight.

Buddy shivered as he heard a high-pitched howl in the distance.

# Search for the Abominable Snowman

## SCARE RATING

With freezing toes and fingers, I check into a hiker's hut on the side of the mountain and huddle by the fire, sipping hot butter tea.

Our expedition into the Himalayan mountains is *not* going well. My team haven't found a scrap of proof that the Migoi, also known as the Abominable Snowman, exists. So far, all we've found here is miles and miles of snow.

"My grandmother told me the story of the Migoi," says our Sherpa and guide, Tashi, his face lit by the flickering flames of the wood stove. "We call him wild man of the snows. Migoi attack our villages."

Tashi holds his nose. "Migoi has a stench so foul, you'll never forget it."

Sometime in the night, I'm woken by thumping outside. I peer outside, but there's nothing there.

*Thump! Thump! Thump!* There's the noise again!

I grab my flashlight and slip out of the hut in the dark and creep onto the narrow mountain path.

There is a tall, dark creature in the distance. Could it be the Abominable Snowman?! Aiming my torch beam at the snow so as not to startle the creature, I follow its huge footprints.

As I get closer, I realize the creature's feet are making the thumping sound, pounding the hard-packed snow. My nostrils curl, picking up its scent of rotten eggs and garbage. *Pee-yew!*

Looking up from the huge footprints under my feet, I raise the beam to keep track of the Migoi.

It's closer than it was and I realize with horror that the Migoi is now moving *toward* me. I back away, but the Abominable Snowman picks me up like a child, holding me firmly under one enormous arm. I kick and scream, but it's too late as he carries me away into the snow-capped mountains.

## SCARY BUT TRUE!

The word *monster* comes from the Latin word *monstrum*, meaning an "unnatural thing or event."

# Unicorn Sighting

## SCARE RATING

Up ahead on the forest path, Emily spotted something quite unbelievable. It looked like a pure-white horse, its mane a magical rainbow of colors topped with a single spiral horn protruding from its forehead.

Emily gasped and crouched behind a tree to get a better look. Could it be . . . a unicorn? A real-life unicorn? This was the best day of her life! The beast shook its massive head, its mane falling down its powerful neck and back. Emily wondered what would happen if she tried to ride it.

Nearby, a twig snapped and a small squirrel snuffled, sniffing the air, its little arms tucked under its chin, completely unfazed by the magical creature grazing beside it.

Suddenly the unicorn stabbed its head toward the squirrel and Emily watched in horror as it skewered the poor little creature with its majestic horn. It tossed its lifeless body aside.

And then it slowly turned its gaze to Emily.

Horn dripping blood, the unicorn snorted, pawed furiously at the ground, and charged straight for Emily.

# It Came from the Deep

## SCARE RATING

Amber *felt* the monster, before she saw it.

As she bopped through the city with her headphones on, the earth shook beneath her feet. Holding on to a lamppost, she noticed people around her running, their mouths open in screams that she couldn't hear as her music played. A storefront window shattered, covering her in glass shards.

A passerby ripped the headphones from her ears and, eyes wild with fear, pointed toward the sky.

"Run!"

The monster, like a cross between a dinosaur and a giant lizard, was so huge it blocked out the midday sun as it stomped down Main Street towering among the skyscrapers. It ripped a

satellite dish from the top of a building and crunched it between its powerful jaws. Amber crouched behind a parked car, praying the monster wouldn't see her.

"Kid, look out!" cried a teenager, sprinting past her.

The monster picked up the SUV Amber was hiding behind with a single claw and tossed it across the street like a toy car.

It roared, flames shooting from its nostrils. Amber sprinted down the street, dodging past building rubble and upturned cars.

The monster was right behind her, its hot breath like rotting fish.

Amber tripped on a pothole and fell to the ground. Still crawling forward on her hands and knees, she looked back to see the underside of a giant, three-toed foot above her, closed her eyes, and screamed.

## SCARY BUT TRUE!

Monsters have been popular in books for hundreds of years. Famous fictional monsters include Count Dracula, Frankenstein's monster, werewolves, mummies, and zombies. Oh, and a guy called Voldemort!

# A Sinking Feeling

## SCARE RATING

Tony rinsed dishes in his uncle's pizza restaurant, Slice. If you asked him (but nobody *ever* did) the place should be shut down by health authorities. There was a cockroach infestation and resident rats who liked to chew on leftover crusts.

Being a dishwasher sure wasn't his dream job, but Tony needed pocket money, and at least Uncle Silvio paid him. Most of the time. Tony took out the plug, but the sink was blocked . . . *again*. He sighed and reached for the drain cleaner, dumping a bunch of chemicals down the plughole. But it didn't help.

"Uncle Silvio, the drain is blocked!" he shouted to his uncle, who was outside sipping coffee, while Tony did all the work.

"Use the plunger!" Silvio shouted back.

Tony pumped hard with the plunger's rubber suction cup. No luck. He reached into the murky water, wiggling his fingers in the clogged pipe.

Something sticky bubbled around his fingers; it felt gooey and gluey. The blob wrapped around his wrist and pulled.

Tony screamed, trying to free himself, but he was quickly pulled into the drain up to his armpit. Uncle Silvio ran inside and grabbed his waist, but the slime creature now had a hold of Tony's entire arm and was sucking him into the drain.

Silvio grabbed a bottle of bleach and squirted it at the blob. It squelched back into the sink, releasing Tony's arm.

Tony cradled his bruised arm, bits of black slime still stuck to it. He took off his dirty apron and threw it on the bench, knowing what he had to do.

"Uncle Silvio, I quit!"

*Inspired by the classic scary movie,* The Blob.

# Finding Nessie

## SCARE RATING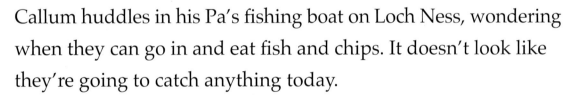

Callum huddles in his Pa's fishing boat on Loch Ness, wondering when they can go in and eat fish and chips. It doesn't look like they're going to catch anything today.

An icy wind whips around his ears and he pulls tighter at his scarf. The fish have taken the day off.

"Nothing's biting today," Pa says, finally. "Shall we pack up, young Callum?"

"Yes!" Callum says eagerly.

Reeling in his line, he feels something tug sharply on the end. A fish!

Callum stands up in the boat and tries to reel in the catch, but it's far too strong for him.

117

"Let me!" Pa says, grabbing the rod. "Whoa! It's a big one!" The rod flies out of Pa's hands.

Moments later, a sea creature emerges from the water with the fishing rod and a hook between its jaws. Callum nearly falls overboard with fright. The creature has a long neck, like a dinosaur, and two humps on its back. It's the size of a bus!

"'Tis the Loch Ness Monster!" shouts Pa. "The legend is true!"

Callum quivers as the monster swims toward their boat, making a honking sound, like it's in pain. Callum shakes in fear, as the monster rocks the boat, baring a row of sharp teeth.

"Take the hook out of its mouth!" shouts Pa as he tries to start the motor. "Can you reach, Callum?"

With a shaking hand, Callum moves his hand closer to the beast, who roars in pain.

"Easy Nessie, don't bite me," Callum whispers, slowly removing the sharp hook from Nessie's mouth.

The monster sinks back down into the water, flicking its tail and disappearing back to the bottom of the lake.

*A large, aquatic, dinosaur-like creature, dubbed the Loch Ness Monster, has been sighted in Loch Ness, Scotland, a deep freshwater lake about 24 miles long.*

# Count Dracula Jr
## SCARE RATING 💀 💀

Vlad was our new exchange student from Transylvania. He was staying with our family for six months. I was excited to meet him, but when he knocked on the door, he looked pale and very ill.

"I was bitten by something before I left home," he explained.

I noticed red welts on his pale skin like awful sunburn, which he tried to cover up with his long sleeves.

"I'll feel better after a good night's sleep," he said, taking his luggage to the guest room and closing the door.

But the next day Vlad didn't get out of bed all day, and the next, and the next.

"Vlad is SO weird," I complained to my mom, but she shushed me loudly.

When he finally did come out of his room, it was midnight and I caught him literally red-handed eating a raw steak from the fridge, gnawing at it hungrily.

I snapped on the light, and he dropped the meat, turning to face me. He had long fangs! Was I about to be his dessert?

Just then, Vlad turned into a small brown bat, flapping around the kitchen light, then straight out the kitchen window, never to be seen again.

# Candyman

## SCARE RATING

After a slumber-party midnight feast and all the scary stories we can think of, my cousin Alice wants to play Candyman and see if we can raise a ghost from the dead.

"Alice, I'm scared," I whisper as we huddle around her bedroom mirror.

"I thought you liked candy," Alice teases. "Fine, I'll do it."

Alice looks into the mirror, her smile fading, expression turning serious.

"— Candyman, Candyman, Candyman, Candyman," she says.

"Wait!" I interrupt. "What if he's evil?"

"—Candyman," Alice finishes. "That's five times. Now look in the mirror."

"Do you see that?" I whisper, gulping as something appears in the glass.

I see the reflection of a man, dressed in a thick trench coat.

Alice holds up her hand to wave and the Candyman does too . . . but his hand is a hook!

Candyman opens his coat to reveal a skinless ribcage, covered by a swarm of bees. I swat at my face, as a bee stings my cheek. Thousands of bees swarm the room now, stinging us over and over. The Candyman steps out of the mirror and we scream.

"The mirror!" cries Alice. "Break the mirror and Candyman will disappear!"

I grab Alice's softball bat from the corner of the room, and swing at the mirror, shattering it to pieces.

Alice's parents rush into the room, turning on the light.

The Candyman has vanished, and all that's left is a room full of broken glass . . . and a single, buzzing bee.

*Inspired by the* Candyman *urban legend.*

# CHAPTER 8

# Don't Go into the Woods

# Scary Selfie

## SCARE RATING

As Sandra trekked into the woods on her first solo hike, she felt a little jittery. But you don't get to be an outdoor-adventure guide if you can't handle a night alone in the wilderness. She told herself to toughen up. Everything would be fine.

As the sun dipped below the trees, Sandra erected her tent and lit a fire for dinner, using just one match. Slurping her instant noodles, she had the odd sensation that she wasn't alone in the forest. Suddenly, a rustling sound in the dark made her jump in fright!

She flashed her torch into the thick pines.

"Hello!" she called out. "Anyone there?"

The rustling stopped, and a squirrel ran across the campsite. Sandra exhaled in relief. Just an animal. Nothing to worry about.

As she snuggled into her sleeping bag, the rustling sounds returned, only this time they were *right outside* her tent.

"Just a squirrel," Sandra whispered, squeezing her eyes shut.

In the morning, Sandra quickly packed up her camp and got back on the trail. Passing a beautiful waterfall, she took out her phone to take a photo. When she opened her album to see how the photo has come out, a chill ran through her body. There were other camping photos . . . that she hadn't taken. Close-up shots of her sleeping in her tent.

Sandra heard a crack behind her, and she turned slowly, finding herself face-to-face with the photographer.

Sandra screamed, and then the woods were silent once more.

## SCARY BUT TRUE!

For hundreds of years, there have been sightings in forested areas of a large, hairy, ape-like creature, roughly 6–9 feet tall (1.8–2.7m), covered in dark hair, with enormous feet. The creature has been nicknamed Bigfoot or Sasquatch. There's even a group called the Bigfoot Field Researchers Organization (BFRO) who search for conclusive proof that Bigfoot exists.

# Spectral Sweetheart

## SCARE RATING

"Legend has it," my friend Caden says as we set up camp for the night in a deserted site, "that years ago a man sprinkled the ashes of his dead wife right here. People say it's haunted."

"Sure it is," I scoff.

"Can you handle a night out here, Gav?" Caden says.

"Can you handle this tent?" I snap. "Otherwise we'll be sleeping in the rain."

Caden sighs and knocks a tent pole into the ground, disappointed by my lack of trembling fear.

"You're no fun."

Later that night, I'm tossing and turning in my sleeping bag when I hear a woman singing outside. I shine a torch outside, but there's no one there. As I lie back down, old-fashioned music starts playing loudly. We're all alone for miles; where is the music coming from? I peer outside again and see a woman dancing in the trees, wearing a long, lacey vintage dress and gloves. Trembling, I wake Caden.

"There . . . there's something out there. A lady. I think she's a ghost."

Caden looks outside, but the woman is gone.

125

"Nice try, Gav," Caden says, before rolling over and going back to sleep.

In the morning, Caden shuffles to the toilet block, and returns quickly.

"Funny joke, Gav," he says.

"What do you mean?" I say, climbing out of the tent and stepping into the clearing.

Around the campfire, the stones have been arranged into a heart shape and the letters B.R.

"You did this, right?" Caden asks.

"I didn't. I swear! I don't even know what B.R. means," I say, puzzled.

"As if you don't know," Caden says. "'B.R.', for Benjamin Roberts. He's the guy who scattered his wife's ashes here a hundred years ago."

## SCARY BUT TRUE!

If you want a ghostly experience, the Hoia-Baciu Forest in Transylvania, Romania, is great for that. Hikers and campers there often feel an unusual sense of foreboding and dread and there have been sightings of unexplained lights and ghostly figures.

# If You Go Down to the Woods Today . . .

## SCARE RATING 💀 💀 💀

The fog had lifted, and I was way ahead—at this pace I was sure to win the school orienteering challenge. My classmates were somewhere, and miles behind my course. I checked my compass and map and headed across the meadow toward the finish line.

In the distance, I spied a large, black, shadowy figure, directly ahead of me and stopped abruptly.

Was it a black bear? I gripped the pepper spray in my pocket. When confronted by a bear, the best thing to do was *not run*.

Slowly, I dropped to the ground, hoping the bear wouldn't charge at me. But as I stared at the creature ahead, I was shocked to see it stand up, with its arms hanging by its sides, just like a person. This wasn't a bear, it was some kind of ape!

The creature moved closer toward me, taking long, bouncing strides. My teeth chattered and I flattened myself to the ground, hoping it

wouldn't see me. The thing was huge—at least seven feet tall—with shaggy black hair all over its body and its muscles bulging.

Breathing rapidly, sweat pouring down my face, I searched my bag for my phone. Forget winning the orienteering challenge, if I got a photo of this strange creature I'd be famous! I focused my screen back toward the ape, but as I did, I felt the ground vibrating beneath me. As I peered through the screen, I watched in horror as the ape creature ran straight at me.

## SCARY BUT TRUE!

The Chupacabra is a legendary cryptid (an animal that might not exist, like a yeti) which is rumored to roam the country-side in South America. The animal's name literally means 'goat sucker' because farmers say the fearsome Chupacabra attacks and drinks the blood of livestock, especially goats.

# The Tower in the Wood
## SCARE RATING 💀 💀 💀 💀

Danish and Amit hiked deep into the overgrown woodland, their voices echoing through the tall trees. Strangely, they hadn't heard a single bird call since they left the main road. The whole woodland was eerily silent.

"Maybe we should turn back," Amit said. "Dad said we shouldn't be out here after dark."

They'd both heard the stories about Sally in the Woods. Years ago, a girl had been trapped in a tower in the heart of the forest, left to starve with no water or food. And starve, in agony, she did. Legend had it, Sally's ghost now stepped out in front of cars at night, causing crashes. There had been six crashes in the past year—all of them unexplained.

"Just a little further," Danish insisted. "I want to find Sally's tower."

After a little while, they found it: the boys stepped out of the brush at the foot of a crumbling stone tower, grown over with vines.

"Let's climb it," Danish said.

"No way!" said Amit. "We found the stupid tower, now let's get out of here."

But Danish went over and pushed hard on the door with his shoulder. Amit eventually gave in and went to help him. Finally, the door gave way and swung open.

In the dim light, Danish trailed his hand along the mossy wall and walked carefully up the broken spiral staircase, Amit following close behind.

They froze halfway up the staircase as an anguished scream from above them pierced the silence. The boys grabbed each other and scrambled back outside—getting the heck out of the woods before Sally found them.

At the base of the tower, their dad waited for the boys, looking cranky.

The boys hurried past their father without a word. They jumped inside the car, where they sat inside, their faces white as sheets.

Dad revved the engine and turned the car onto the road. "Boys, I told you to be back at—" Dad slammed his feet on the brakes and the car skidded on the road as a girl in rags stepped out in front of the car.

*Based on the story of Sally in the Wood.*

# The Prankster's Mistake
## SCARE RATING 💀 💀 💀 💀

Kai snuck away from the campfire sing-along and back to his cabin. He went to his luggage to retrieve the scary hockey-mask he'd packed to terrify his friend Jackson. They'd been pranking each other all summer, and this trick was going to be epic.

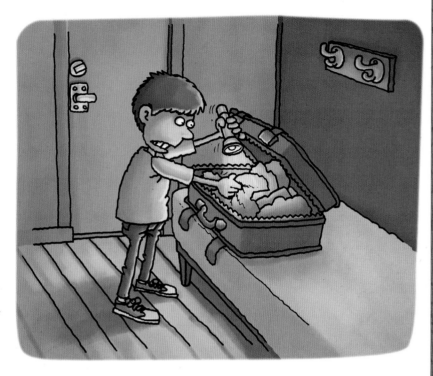

Kai flicked the light switch but nothing happened. Kai sighed and grabbed his flashlight. The camp was run on generator power, and it had shorted out twice this summer already. So annoying. He continued searching through his bag, now with only the weak flashlight beam. It wasn't in the side pocket anymore, where he'd carefully packed it. He rummaged through the bag, digging through his stuff, before moving the suitcase onto the floor. But there was no mask. Strange.

When he heard a slow knock at the cabin door, Kai instantly knew what had happened. He opened it to find Jackson, wearing his lost hockey mask.

"Very funny, Jackson," he said. "You can take the mask off now. I know it's you."

In the dark cabin, it was hard to make out, but Kai suddenly noticed how much taller this person was than Jackson. And was that a real knife in his hand?

Kai backed away, tripping on his suitcase, as the man behind the mask growled: "Who's Jackson?"

## SCARY BUT TRUE!

Braley Pond is Virginia's most haunted campsite. The site of several murders, campers say they've heard children's voices and seen spirits hovering above the water.

# Hide and Seek
## SCARE RATING 💀 💀 💀 💀

"1…2…3…4…5—" calls our Scout Leader, Mr. Ramirez, as we scatter into the woods for the best hiding spots.

My best friend, Jasper, crawls into a hollowed-out log, which is teeming with bugs.

"Come in here, Carlos!" Jasper whispers. "There's plenty of room."

"No thanks," I say, shuddering. I crouch behind a fallen tree nearby and wait.

"Ready or not, here I come!" Mr. Ramirez shouts.

I try to stay still as he finds each kid one by one. He finds me huddled behind the tree and I come out with my palms up.

"Any idea where Jasper is, Carlos?" Mr. Ramirez asks.

My eyes must flick over to the hollow log, and he goes right to it.

"Jasper!" Mr. Ramirez calls. "Come out, come out, wherever you are!"

**133**

Mr. Ramirez crawls inside the log, and comes out with a puzzled look on his face. "Jasper's not there," he says.

I look at the log, confused. "Yes, he is!" I say, rushing into the dark tunnel of the log. But, apart from slimy and slithery insects, it's empty.

We spend the next half hour searching the forest, calling out Jasper's name. But he's vanished. Mr. Ramirez calls the state police.

"Search and rescue teams are on the way," says Mr. Ramirez, peering up at the darkening sky. "Let's head back to camp; no use us getting lost out here, too."

A cold, sinking feeling floods my body. Jasper was wearing only a T-shirt and shorts. He didn't have food or water. How long would he last on his own out here? As the troop trudges over a hill, I duck behind a tree and circle back to the log, alone, to find my friend. As I approach the log, I hear a scratching sound inside, and my hopes lift.

"Jasper!" I shout, crawling into the dark, moss-covered tunnel.

An icy, pale hand reaches out and grabs my wrist, pulling me into the darkness.

# Out of the Rain

## SCARE RATING

The thunderstorm batters the forest, peppering Rex and his dad with hailstones. A purple crack of lightning lights up the sky, leaving them shaking in fear.

"We need to find cover!" Rex shouts.

"Over there?" his Dad shouts back, pointing to an abandoned cabin a few hundred yards away.

*So much for their father-son camping trip.*

They bolt for cover, hailstones bouncing off their backs.

Rex pushes the rotting cabin door open. Inside, there is a horrible stench; the single room is dusty and filthy. Rex picks up a rusting metal can of mystery food, still sitting on the table.

"Dinner?" he jokes.

As their eyes adjust to the dim light, Rex feels uneasy. Something about this cabin isn't quite right.

There's a splatter of a dark liquid across the wall. On the bed is an old-fashioned rifle and a hunting knife. The bed looks soaked in the same dark liquid.

Rex touches it, and his fingers come away sticky. Blood?

Dad picks up the rifle.

"Wow, this thing is *old*," he says.

"Don't!" says Rex. "Put it down."

"Relax, Rex, this place has been abandoned for at least a hundred years. It's practically a museum."

Dad switches on his flashlight, shining the beam around the room to reveal bullet holes in the walls and a message written in the dust:

## GET OUT NOW

Dad screams and Rex scrambles for the front door, a bullet skimming the side of his head.

## SCARY BUT TRUE!

The Dering Woods in Kent, England, are also known as the Screaming Woods because of the blood-curdling screams heard in the forest late at night.

# The Night Marchers
## SCARE RATING

"It's not safe to go walking at night here," Dad said, zipping me and my sister Kiki tightly into our sleeping bags.

We were camping in a dense rain forest in Hawaii, near a sacred waterfall. In the morning, we planned to hike there and go swimming—I couldn't wait!

"Be careful of the Night Marchers," Dad whispered, looking over his shoulder, as if the ancient warrior spirits could actually *hear* him. I didn't believe the stories that a bunch of ghostly

warriors marched around at night, capturing anyone who dared even to look at them.

"That's just a myth," I said, but Dad gave me a stern look.

"It most certainly is not," he said. "Stay in your tent until it's light out. And if you see them . . ."

"Never look at them!" Kiki and I said together, giggling.

"That's right," Dad said, tickling Kiki and making her squeal. "Or they'll getcha!"

I woke up early and stuck my head out of the tent. Technically, it was still dark outside, but the birds were twittering, and Dad was snoring in his tent. I pulled on my swimsuit and headed toward the waterfall, planning to take a flying leap off the rock and into the cool water.

In the distance, the low sound of drums beating stopped me in my tracks. Someone blew into a conch shell.

What was that about? Hair prickled on my arms as I remembered Dad's strict warning. In the dim morning light, a line of lit torches headed toward me through the jungle.

I ducked behind a fern as a procession of warriors emerged from the mist, wearing bone necklaces, and carrying sharp, barbed spears.

Suddenly, the procession wheeled sharply to the left—heading straight for me! I jumped out of my hiding spot and tripped, falling to my knees. Shaking, I looked up to find myself staring right into the black eyes of a Night Marcher.

As a shot of fiery pain ran through my eyes, I remembered Dad's warning: *Never look at a Night Marcher.*

*Based on the legend of the* Hawaiian Night Marchers.

## SCARY BUT TRUE!

The Dyatlov Pass incident refers to the unsolved deaths of nine Russian hikers in 1959. Something caused the experienced campers to flee their tents at night in sub-zero temperatures. Six died of hypothermia, the other three of internal physical trauma, with no evidence of injuries. What exactly happened to the hikers that night has never been uncovered.

# WARNING!

These stories might give you nightmares!

Are you sure you want to continue?

# The Legend of Hanako-San

## SCARE RATING 💀💀💀💀💀

"You're the new kid in school, so you *have* to do it," says Ryosuke.

He pulls me up the stairs to the third floor and shoves me inside the girls' bathroom, slamming the door behind me. I push back, but he's leaning against it from the other side, and it won't budge. I'm trapped. A fluorescent bulb flickers in the dim bathroom. There are no windows, no escape.

With a shaking fist, I knock three times on the third stall down, just like Ryosuke instructed, the sound bouncing off the damp, tiled walls.

"Are you there, Hanako-San?" I ask, my voice trembling.

Outside, Ryosuke is laughing, and the bell rings for class, but inside the bathroom, it's eerily silent. As the seconds tick past, relief floods my body. It's just a stupid joke. Of course the ghost of Hanako-San isn't real.

"It didn't work!" I shout to Ryosuke, who doesn't answer.

As I press against the jammed door to get out, something in the mirror catches my eye. A small white hand is reaching out from under the third stall and the door slowly creaks open. My mouth is dry, and I'm glued to the spot with fear. In the stall is a small girl in a red shirt, long dark hair covering her face.

"Ryosuke! Let me out!" I scream and frantically bang on the bathroom door, but it's stuck. Where is Ryosuke? Has he gone to class and left me?

The girl walks slowly toward me, lifting up her hair to reveal eyes trickling with blood.

*Inspired by the* Legend of Hanako-San, *a popular Japanese ghost story.*

# The Cupboard in the Cellar
## SCARE RATING 💀💀💀💀

"Martin! Where are you?" shouted Valeria. Her brother had run off after lunch and hadn't been seen for hours. She was determined to find him so they could go for a swim in the lake.

They were visiting her great-uncle Lucas; he lived in a rambling old mansion, and there were lots of good hiding spots.

Too good.

"Maybe he's been taken by the monster in the cellar," said Great-Uncle Lucas, looking grim.

"Very funny, Lucas," said Valeria.

Great-Uncle Lucas was a notorious liar. When he was just a boy he had sworn his best friend had been eaten by a monster in the cellar, but he had locked the beast in a cupboard and hidden the key—still to this day he wouldn't tell anyone where it was. He liked scaring Valeria and Martin with silly, made-up stories. His friend had never been found, though; it was a sad story, actually.

After looking everywhere else she could think of, Valeria stomped down to the cellar, her chest tightening as she descended the stone steps. Great-Uncle Lucas's tall tales had made her afraid of the cellar. She walked through the small, damp room lined with old bottles and lit with a dim bulb.

"Martin!" she called, her voice bouncing around the cramped space. "Come out now! Let's go for a swim."

"I'm here!" Martin cried from behind the huge, antique cupboard. He was trying to grasp something just out of arm's reach.

"Can you reach my ball, Valeria?" Martin asked, dusting cobwebs and dirt from his T-shirt.

She slid behind the cupboard, grabbed the ball, and accidentally knocked a piece of plaster from the crumbling wall.

A silver key fell to the ground.

She stood in front of the locked cupboard with Martin, the key heavy in her palm.

"You don't think . . ." she said, looking at the cupboard.

"Should we open it?" Martin said.

"What about the monster?" said Valeria.

"That's just a story."

He was right, of course. Valeria slid the key into the rusty lock, and turned it ever so gently.

It was too late when she realized what she'd done.

As if something was waking from a long slumber, a low growl came from the cupboard. It grew louder and louder and then the doors flew open.

## SCARY BUT TRUE!

The Beast of Bodmin Moor is a phantom panther-like wildcat that allegedly slinks around Cornwall in England. It was first sighted in 1978, along with reports of farmers discovering mutilated, dead livestock. Rumor has it the wildcat was set free or escaped from an illegal private zoo, but scientists say there's no proof the beast even exists.

# New Best Friend

## SCARE RATING 💀💀💀💀

"I miss my old school friends," I say to Mom. My new town is quiet compared to the city. It's lonely and boring.

"Let's go to the park," Mom suggests.

"Can we go for ice cream after?" I say.

"Sure we can."

The park is deserted, windy, and cold. Mom sits on a bench with her phone, and I swing by myself.

"Can I play?" a voice asks.

A girl my age is standing by the swings, wearing a checkered dress with a rip in the hem.

"Sure!" I say.

She sits on the swing beside me and begins to swing.

"My name is Molly," she says.

"I'm Lauren. We just moved here. I don't have any friends yet."

"I'll be your friend," says Molly.

She holds out her small hand and I take it. It's ice-cold; she should be wearing a jacket. It's freezing out.

"Wait here," I say. I jump off the swing and run toward Mom.

"Can my new friend join us for ice cream?" I ask, excitedly.

Mom looks over my shoulder at the swings. "What friend?"

I spin around and see that Molly has vanished, the swings still moving gently.

"I think I know why this park is deserted," says Mom, looking at Google on her phone.

"A girl went missing here 50 years ago today. She came out to meet her friends and never came home."

# Zombie High
## SCARE RATING

Principal Atkins makes an announcement over the loudspeaker: "Students! McArthur Elementary is on immediate lockdown— follow procedure and listen to your teac—" Mr. Atkins' voice cuts out and my best friend Annie squeezes my hand tightly.

Mrs. Dao locks our classroom door.

"Children, please hide now," she says, her voice shaking.

I scramble under my desk as Mrs. Dao draws the curtains.

Outside, the zombie horde have arrived. Surrounding the school, zombies shake at the school's metal chain-link fence.

"Zombies!" I whisper to Annie, and her grip gets even tighter.

"Stay calm," says Mrs. Dao. "Help is on the way."

It's hard to stay calm as we hear the fence crash into the school yard and the moaning of a thousand undead corpses trample across the football field. The zombies reach our classroom and scratch at the glass with rotten fingernails.

"I'm scared," Annie says, her eyes filling with tears.

"Me too."

The glass shatters, and zombies climb over each other into the room, clawing for their next meal . . . *us.*

Manny, one of our friends, crawls out from under his desk and snatches the keys from Mrs. Dao.

"Don't open the door!" she screams.

But we were no safer in here than out there. At least outside we're not cornered.

Manny yanks the door open and disappears into the chaos in the hall.

"Run!" I shout, grabbing Annie's hand, but she's glued to the spot with fear. I pull her arm desperately, but a zombie is shuffling toward her, teeth gnashing, skin falling from its bones.

I let go of Annie's hand just as a zombie bites into her arm. Running down the hall, I find a hiding spot behind the lockers where I wait, silently, until, finally, everything goes quiet.

I peer around the lockers. A pair of familiar brown shoes squeak on the floor as they move down the hall.

"Annie?" I whisper, ducking my head out.

Annie lets out a horrible groan, chomping her teeth and shuffling toward me with her blood-stained arms outstretched.

# Bloody Mary

## SCARE RATING

"Say Bloody Mary three times into the mirror," says Gabriela. "You're not *scared*, are you?"

"Of course not," Laura says quickly. "Why would I be scared?"

Laura's skin is clammy and her stomach churns. They creep down the dark hall to the bathroom, floorboards creaking, trying not to wake Gabriela's parents. Gabriela ushers Laura into the room and shuts the door quietly behind them. Gabriela shines a flashlight and pushes Laura in front of the large mirror.

Laura looks at her own reflection in the mirror.

Laura's lips quiver; she's close to tears. "What will happen if I call Bloody Mary?" she asks.

"You'll summon the ghost of Bloody Mary—a murderous witch who died 100 years ago," whispers Gabriela dramatically,

holding the flashlight so that the light shines under her chin.

"Why would I want to do that?" Laura asks, staring at her friend in shock.

"Don't be a wimp," Gabriela says, "it's fun, just do it."

Laura takes a deep breath for courage and chants the words in a low whisper, her voice shaking. "Bloody Mary," she says, "Bloody Mary, Bloody Mary . . ."

At first, nothing happens and Laura feels silly for being so scared.

The girls look at each other and laugh at how nervous they had been.

Laura watches as Gabriela glances back at the mirror and her eyes grow wide.

A ghastly witch stands behind them in the reflection, her skin slashed and eyes white.

Bloody Mary smiles, showing off sharp teeth, blood oozing down her chin. She lets out a long cackle. Laura screams as the witch extends her long, bony arms from the mirror, reaching for her with filthy yellow claws.

# The Moaning Tree
## SCARE RATING

After a long day of hiking, Jenny's family were fast asleep inside their tents in the state forest. But not Jenny. Jenny desperately needed to pee, but it was the middle of the night and she was terrified to venture into the dark woods on her own.

When she couldn't hold on any longer, she grabbed her flashlight and walked slowly down the dark path, away from the campsite. Branches creaked, leaves rustled, and animals scurried; she heard a low moan coming from an ancient, gnarled pine that her brother, Craig, called The Moaning Tree. He swore that hundreds of years ago it had been used to hang lawbreakers from the nearby town. With so much death, everything around The Moaning Tree had died with it;

bushes had turned white, flowers had shriveled and died, and the grass was long gone.

Jenny shivered as she approached the ghostly, twisted pine; she had no choice but to pass under it on her way to the toilet block. She held her breath, breaking into a run, her heart thudding. As she passed, the moaning grew louder, then it turned into a powerful scream—like the desperate cries of a hundred people all at once.

Underneath its branches, Jenny came to an abrupt halt, like her legs were stuck. She saw something start to materialize from the branch. It was a noose! A ghostly apparition appeared beside it.

The spirit beckoned her with its otherworldly fingers and rasped, "Join us, return with us to the underworld tonight!"

She screamed and tried to run, but something was restraining her. It was a tree root! Unfurling itself from the ghastly tree it had wrapped itself around her ankle and was pulling her slowly toward it.

# Earthly Endeavors
## SCARE RATING 💀 💀 💀 💀 💀

Opening my eyes, I see nothing but blackness. I reach upward, my palms hitting the satin cushioning just over my head. I try to sit up, but my body is trapped tightly in a box! My heart swells with fear as I desperately grope the tight space around me. I pat my clothes . . . Why am I wearing my formal suit? I search my memory—the last thing I remember I was in bed, ill, burning up with fever.

And then nothing.

The tightly enclosed bed, the complete silence in the dark. A chill of terror runs through me as I make the grisly realization: I'm trapped underground in a coffin. My family has mistakenly buried me alive!

I push as hard on the coffin lid as my weakened arms allow, but the box is sealed tight. I kick, cry out, and push at the lid until my hands ache and my voice is hoarse. But there's nobody deep down in the earth to hear me.

My breath comes in ragged gasps; I'm quickly running out of air! I twist in the box, trying to break free, screaming, clawing my fingernails down the coffin lid, taking my last gasps of air.

As I'm about to give up hope, I hear a sound, the best sound I could possibly imagine: the metal tip of a shovel hitting the top of my coffin.

## SCARY BUT TRUE!

Under Iceland's Child Protection Act, children under 12 are not allowed outdoors after dark (8pm), unless accompanied by an adult—otherwise they're taken to the police station for collection by their parents!

# Alien Invader
## SCARE RATING

Bailey was part of the first colony to settle on Mars's International Space Station.

"I'm going to the greenhouse," he shouted to Lotte in the control room.

As he approached the airlock, he made sure to follow procedure. Mars's carbon dioxide atmosphere was poisonous to humans and nobody could leave the station without full protective gear and oxygen tanks.

In the greenhouse, Bailey checked the lettuce patch, shocked to find most of the plants had been eaten.

But, as far as Bailey knew, he and his three fellow astronauts were the only living beings on the red planet.

Bailey touched a half-eaten head of lettuce, a string of gooey, sticky liquid trailing from his gloves. He ran to the control room to tell Lotte, who immediately locked the greenhouse hatch door.

"Whatever ate those lettuces might not be friendly," said Lotte. "We can't take any chances."

That night, as Bailey lay in his bed, reading, he heard a strange clicking sound. On the foot of his bed was an alien creature, with eight spindly legs and giant bug eyes staring straight at him.

The alien pounced on his chest, pinning him down and spat a thick, sticky web around his face and mouth.

Even if Bailey did scream, no one would hear him.

# Ghostly GPS

## SCARE RATING

"How much?" Rich asked the car dealer, as he walked around the gray SUV.

"It's $5,000, final offer," the dealer said. "Listen, buddy, it's getting late, do you wanna buy the car or not?"

"How about $4,500," Rich bargained.

"Deal," the car dealer said, shaking Rich's hand. "Just one thing," he added, "this car belonged to Fatz McPhee."

Rich shrugged. Fatz McPhee was a gangster and convicted murderer who'd recently passed away. Who cared? He was getting a sweet deal on the car and it would be a cool story, too. Rumor had it that Fatz often used his car during his crime sprees; some of his victims' DNA was even found in it, but never a body. Not until the last one.